[Reprinted from THE JOURNAL OF AMERICAN FOLK-LORE
October–December, 1917.]

KASKA TALES.[1]

BY JAMES A. TEIT.

CONTENTS.

	PAGE		PAGE
Preface	427	13. The Sisters who married Stars	457
1. Story of Beaver	429	14. The Man who cohabited with his Sister	459
2. Origin of the Earth	441	15. Story of the Water-Man	460
3. The Great Flood	442	16. The Deceitful Wife	461
4. Origin of Fire, and Origin of Death	443	17. The Owl-Woman	462
5. Raven, or Big-Crow	444	18. The Dog-Man and Dog-Children	463
6. Big-Man (Déne Tco')	444	19. Story of Lynx-Man	464
7. The Brothers, Big-Man, and the Giants	445	20. The Fog-Man	465
8. The Giants and the Boys	448	21. Rabbit-Man (Ga.'tcoeze')	467
9. Bladder-Head Boy; or, The Monster that ate People	450	22. Wolverene	469
10. The Kaska Man who made Whales	451	23. Wolverene and his Wives	470
11. War with the Swan People	453	24. Wolverene and Wolf	471
12. The Deserted Woman	455	25. Story of the Baby stolen by Wolverene	471

PREFACE.

THE following collection of tales or traditions is from the Kaska of the northern interior of British Columbia. The Kaska and Tahltan are closely related tribes of the Nahani division of the Athapascan stock, and occupy territories adjacent to each other. The Tahltan inhabit the whole region of the upper Stikine River, and extend easterly to Dease Lake and River, where they meet the Kaska, who claim the country from there down to the Liard. The Tahltan are thus chiefly on the Pacific drainage slope, and the Kaska altogether on the Arctic slope. Owing to their location, the Tahltan have an abundance of salmon in their country, while the Kaska have none. Both tribes live

[1] The present collection of Kaska tales, together with another one of Tahltan tales, was collected by Mr. J. A. Teit in the seasons of 1912 and 1915 in the region of Stikine River, British Columbia. These two seasons of field-work were devoted to a general ethnological investigation of the Tahltan and Kaska Indians, under the auspices of the Geological Survey of Canada. The present publication embraces the mythological results of the trips. Other aspects of the ethnology collected by Mr. Teit will be published by the Geological Survey from time to time in the form of special monographs. To facilitate the appearance of Mr. Teit's Tahltan and Kaska tales, the Geological Survey of Canada has authorized its Division of Anthropology to intrust their publication to the American Folk-Lore Society. — E. SAPIR, Head of Division of Anthropology, Geological Survey of Canada.

chiefly by hunting and trapping, but the Kaska depend more on the chase than do the Tahltan. Large game-animals are abundant, consisting of moose, caribou, sheep, goat, and bear. Marmots are plentiful in certain parts, and buffalo are said to have been fairly numerous at one time in the more eastern sections of the country.

The Kaska are entirely surrounded by Athapascan tribes, while the Tahltan are neighbors of tribes of two other stocks; viz., the Tlingit to the northwest and west, and the Niska and Kitksan tribes of the Tsimshian stock to the southwest. To the south the Sikani, Carrier, and Chilcotin tribes of the Athapascan stock separate the Tahltan and Kaska from the Shuswap and Lillooet, the nearest tribes of the interior Salish. Owing largely to their position, the Tahltan had a great deal of intercourse with the Tlingit, much more than with any other people. Intercourse and trading were chiefly by way of Stikine River. Trade was in the hands of the Tlingit of Wrangell and vicinity, who annually transported goods by canoe up the river to the head of canoe navigation, a little above Telegraph Creek and close to the headquarters of the Tahltan. The people of the latter tribe acted as middlemen in passing coast products inland, and inland products coastward. The main trade-route between the far east (the Mackenzie valley and the plains) and the Pacific coast in this part of British Columbia lay through the Tahltan and Kaska territory, and there is evidence of a number of cultural features having penetrated a long distance in both directions along that route. Here, as in other parts of the west, the main trade-routes lay as nearly east and west as the physical features of the country allowed; while other routes running north and south within the interior were unimportant, notwithstanding the fact that the nature of the country generally was favorable for travel and intercourse.

It may be expected that dissemination of tales has occurred chiefly along the main trade-routes, where intercourse between the tribes was most frequent and closest. Hence throughout the interior, dissemination of tales has followed east and west lines rather than north and south. As the same conditions as to routes prevailed in the southern interior as in the northern, it seems probable that a number of the incidents in tales of the Tahltan and Kaska which correspond with those in tales of the interior Salish have not passed directly from Athapascan to Salish tribes, or *vice versâ*, but have reached both from the same eastern and western sources,—chiefly, it seems, the latter. The Tahltan assert that in the old trading-rendezvous on the upper Stikine, members of the two tribes associated there for weeks together, and that one of the features of meeting was story-telling. Tahltan *raconteurs* told their stories one day, and Tlingit told theirs the following day. Sometimes they thus told stories turn about for weeks. Occasionally the tribes competed in story-telling to see which had the most stories. As a result, it came to be acknowledged that the Tlingit had considerably more stories than the Tahltan. In this way, it is said, the Tahltan learned Tlingit stories, and *vice versâ*.

It is therefore not surprising to find many elements of Tlingit origin in Tahltan tales. It seems that most stories of the Raven cycle, and many other tales, have been borrowed almost in their entirety. On the other hand, the Kaska tales show much less indication of Tlingit influence, and probably a little more of influence from the east. On the whole, they are probably more purely Athapascan. The importance of the chase (especially hunting of caribou) is reflected in the tales of both tribes. Fishing is not prominent, excepting in tales borrowed from the Tlingit. Root-digging and berrying, features often referred to in Salish tales, are almost entirely absent. Tales of European origin appear to be altogether unknown. I inquired for such tales as those of Petit Jean, John the Bear, and others, but without result. About one hundred and fifty themes, episodes, and incidents occurring in tales of the interior Salish (chiefly Shuswap), regarding which I made inquiry, I failed to obtain among the Tahltan, and there are also many others that are absent.

All the Tahltan tales, with the exception of six, were collected during the course of my work among the tribe in 1912. Almost all of them were obtained from Tuuʹts ("strong rocks"), also known as "Dandy Jim," of the Nahlin clan of the Raven phratry of the Tahltan. He was selected by the tribe as the best-qualified person to give me information on their general ethnology, mythology, and so on. The other six tales were obtained at Telegraph Creek in 1915 from Jim and others. The Kaska tales were collected at the foot of Dease Lake in 1915, my informants being Tsonakeʹl, also known as Albert Dease, and his wife Nettie Mejadeʹsse, both members of the Kaska tribe. In every case I collected all the tales my informants knew.

Historic traditions, such as tales of war-expeditions and migrations, are not included in the present collection. I have included a number of variants of incidents in the text. I have added some explanatory notes where these seemed to be required. The comparative notes, excepting those referring to the interior Salish, Chilcotin, and some of the Tsetsaʹut notes, were added by the Editor of the Journal.

1. STORY OF BEAVER.

A long time ago, when all the animals were people, Beaver was a great transformer. He travelled along a wide trail that was much used. Along the trail were many monsters that preyed on people. He came to a place where people always disappeared. Wolverene killed them. His house was at the foot of a glacier, between two rocky bluffs. The glacier was very slippery, and people crossing it slid down to the bottom, where they were transfixed on a spear placed there by Wolverene. As soon as something touched the spear, Wolverene knew it, and came out at once. If they were dead, he carried the bodies home; if they were only wounded, he killed them. His house was full of peoples' bones. Beaver went down this slide, and, cutting his lips with the spear so that they bled, pretended to be dead. Wolverene knew something had been caught, and came out smiling and very happy. When he saw Beaver, he said, "What a large beaver!" Then he laughed, and said, "I have caught this clever man." He carried the body home and put it down in his house. He had four flensing-knives. He used one after another, but they would not cut Beaver's skin. Then he searched for the fourth knife. Beaver knew that this knife would cut him, so he opened his eyes to see where he might find a stick. One of Wolverene's children noticed him, and called out, "Father, the Beaver has opened his eyes!" Wolverene answered, "You are mistaken. How can a dead man open his eyes?" Beaver jumped up and seized a stick, with which he broke Wolverene's arms and legs. He killed him, and put his body before the fire to roast. He also killed all Wolverene's children, and treated their bodies likewise.[1]

Beaver went on, and came to a bluff overlooking a deep creek. He heard a dog barking below the cliff. He listened, and approached cautiously. Presently he saw a man on the top of the cliff, and went to him. This was Sheep-Man, who killed people by pushing them over the cliff. His wife attracted them by barking like a dog, and any who were not killed outright by the fall were clubbed by her at the bottom of the cliff. When Beaver reached Sheep-Man, the latter said, "Look at the sheep down below!" Beaver said, "You look first, you saw them first." They quarrelled as to who should look over the brink first. At last Sheep-Man looked, and Beaver at once pushed him over. He was killed by the fall.[2] When Sheep-Man's wife heard the thud of something falling at the base of the cliff, she ran out quickly, and began to club the man before she noticed that it was her own husband. She then looked up and saw Beaver, who threw a rock at her head and killed her. *This is why the head of the mountain-sheep is so small between the horns; and the tongues of sheep are black because they once ate men.*

Beaver travelled on, and came to a large camp of Sheep people. The women were good, and called to him, "Why do you come this way?" He answered, "I am looking for friends who have passed

[1] Bellacoola (Boas, JE 1 : 86, Sagen 250), Eskimo (Boas, BAM 15 : 176), Loucheux (Camsell-Barbeau, JAFL 28 : 255), Tsetsa'ut (Boas, JAFL 10 : 46).

[2] Chilcotin (Farrand, JE 2 : 26), Pend d'Oreille (Teit, MAFLS 11 : 116), Sahaptin (Farrand-Mayer, MAFLS 11 : 152); see also RBAE 31 : 803.

along this trail." The Sheep men followed him, and he ran among bluffs and rocks. It became dark; but they pursued him, just the same, by scenting him. He went down a steep place, and the Sheep did not know exactly which way he had gone. There his trail was a sheer cliff. They called out, "How did you get down?" and Beaver directed them to the sheer cliff. The Sheep then all ran over the cliff and were killed.[1]

In the morning an old woman and girl arrived there. The woman proposed to marry Beaver, and had told the girl that when she slept with him, she (the girl) must club Beaver while he was asleep. Beaver refused the request of the women, and killed them both.

Beaver proceeded on his journey, and, after crossing a mountain, sat down on the trail. He saw a man coming, carrying a stick with a hook at the end. This was Marten-Man, who killed people (by hooking them between the legs). Beaver placed a piece of sheep's flesh between his legs and sat still. Marten asked many questions of Beaver. They conversed together and told stories to each other. Meanwhile Marten pushed his stick underneath the snow and hooked the meat. Beaver ran away, and Marten chased him. As he ran, Beaver dropped pieces of sheep's fat. Marten could not catch him, and turned back to his camp. He said to his wife, "I have lost some very fat game. The fat kept dropping from him as he ran. We will shift camp, and I will track him." Next morning Marten tracked Beaver, and his wife and children followed behind. Beaver lay in wait for Marten, and killed him. He cut off one arm, and covered the rest of the body with snow. Then, making a camp, he scattered pieces of sheep's fat about, and put Marten's arm on a hook to roast. He had just hidden himself when Marten's family appeared. The children were delighted, saying, "Father has killed some fat game. See the camp, and the arm roasting, and the pieces of fat scattered about!" They ran around on their snowshoes, laughing, and gathering up the pieces of fat. When Beaver appeared, the eldest boy was going to shoot him with an arrow; but Beaver called out, "Don't! I am going to marry your sister." His mother took hold of his arm, and said, "Don't shoot! He will be your sister's husband." Beaver said, "I will make a big fire, so that the meat will roast quickly." They did not know that it was Marten's arm. Beaver brought in some wood covered with snow and put it on the fire, which now became smoky and nearly went out. He asked the mother and children to get down on their hands and knees and blow on the fire. When they did so, Beaver clubbed them, and killed them all excepting the youngest child, who ran away and climbed a tree. Beaver could not catch him,

[1] See Kutenai (Boas, BBAE 59 : 269, and notes 311 [Blackfoot, Shoshoni, Tsetsa'ut, Uinta Ute]).

so he transformed him into the animal marten, saying, "*Henceforth you shall be an ordinary marten, and shall eat rabbits and mice. You shall never again eat men.*"

Beaver continued his journey along the trail.[1] When near a small, round lake, he saw that a giant was following him. He went around the lake, and the giant chased him. Beaver ran round and round the lake, the giant behind him. The latter could not catch him, and began to slacken his pace. He said to Beaver, "How can I catch you?" Beaver answered, "Make ready everything required for frying and cooking my meat, then make a snare, set it, and catch me." The giant did as advised. Beaver put a large tree-stump in the snare and hid in the brush. The giant felt something in his snare, and began to pull on the line. It was very heavy, and he gave a mighty tug. The stump gave way, and, flying up, struck him on the forehead. The wound bled much, and the giant licked and swallowed the blood as it ran down his face. He was very tired and hungry, for he had chased Beaver all day. He sat down, and thought, "What shall I eat?" He thought of eating his ears, but said, "No! if I eat my ears, I shall spoil my hearing." He thought of his nose, and said, "No! if I eat my nose, I shall no longer be able to smell." He thought of all the different parts of his body, and at last of his privates. He could not think of their being of much use, so he cut them off and ate them. He felt sick, and said to himself, "I am getting very sleepy." He was dying, but did not know it. He lay down and died.

Beaver continued his travels, and came to the edge of a large river.[2] Happening to look round, he saw another giant coming. He took off his clothes, and painted himself with the white powdery substance that covers the outside bark of cottonwood-trees. He looked like a ghost. He put little sticks in his eyes to keep the eyelids open, and stood rigid and immovable alongside the trail. As the giant approached, he said, "That game looks very strange." He took his axe and made as if he would strike; but Beaver never moved, or winked an eye. The giant said, "This cannot be game." The giant tickled him in different parts of the body, but Beaver neither moved nor laughed. The giant said again, "This is funny." He poked his finger in Beaver's anus, and then smelled of it, saying, "Well, this smells like game, but the body does not act or look like game. This is very strange." He departed wondering. Beaver ran away and climbed a tree. The giant changed his mind, and returned to examine him again. When he arrived at the place and found that he was gone, he said, "I am very sorry I did not hit him with my axe. It was surely game." He followed the tracks

[1] Also known to the Tahltan.

[2] The following incident is also known to the Tahltan. See Tsetsa'ut (Boas, JAFL 10 : 4c).

to the bottom of a tree near the water-edge, but never looked up into the tree. He saw Beaver's reflection in the river, and said, "There he is!" He struck at the reflection with his axe. Then he moved to the side and struck again. The giant kept this up for a long time, and was completely soaked with the splashing of the water. He had about made up his mind that he could not kill him, when Beaver laughed. The giant looked up into the tree and saw him.[1] He said, "I will shoot you," and he put an arrow on his bow. Beaver called, "Don't! If you shoot me, I shall fall into the river, and you will lose me." The giant said, "I will fire the tree;" and Beaver answered, "You mustn't. If you do that, you will burn me up, and lose all my fat." The giant said, "I will chop down the tree;" and Beaver answered, "No! if you do that, the tree will fall into the water, and you will lose me." The giant said, "Then how shall I get you?" Beaver answered, "Get a long pole and put a noose at the end and catch me." The giant agreed to this. Beaver said, "Go up on yonder hill and cut a pole." The giant went up, and, seeing a good-looking pole, called out to Beaver, "Will this one do?" Beaver answered, "No, go farther! that is not the right kind." Beaver kept on urging the giant to go farther, until he reached the top of the mountain. The giant showed a pole from there; and Beaver called out, "That one will do, now put a noose on it and get everything ready." Beaver then came down out of the tree, and swam across the river. When the giant came back, he missed Beaver, and said, "He has got away. I am very sorry I did not shoot him." Beaver talked to him from across the river. The giant asked him, "How did you get across there?" and Beaver answered, "I made my blanket into a canoe by tying it up and putting a board in the bottom." The giant did this, and when nearly across began to sink. He called out, "Help! I am sinking!" and pushed out the pole he had cut for Beaver to catch it and pull him out. Beaver took hold of the pole and pushed the giant under water and drowned him.

Beaver now made a canoe and went down the river. He saw smoke and a camp, and put ashore and tied up his canoe. This was the camp of Woodchuck, who ate men. He said to Beaver, "I am a good man, and treat my guests well. I shall cook, that you may eat, for you must be hungry." He cooked a mixture of human and other flesh. Beaver knew the human flesh and would not eat it. Woodchuck became angry, jumped on him, and scratched him. They fought a long time; and Beaver killed Woodchuck and threw his body into the river. He then burned his lodge and all his belongings.

Continuing down the river, Beaver reached the camp of Bushtail-

[1] See Boas BBAE 59 : 305, note 3 (Assiniboin, Bellacoola, Blackfoot, Caddo, Chilcotin, Comox, Haida, Kutenai, Kwakiutl, Nootka, Ojibwa, Osage, Quinault, Shuswap, Thompson, Tsimshian). Also known to Tahltan.

Rat, who was also a cannibal. He said to Beaver, "Be my guest; I am a good man, and will treat you well. I will cook food for you." He cooked a kettleful of flesh, which when done he served on a dish. He put the human flesh on the side of the dish next to Beaver, who did not touch it, but ate only from the other side of the dish. Rat was very angry, and he and his wife jumped on Beaver. They fought a long time and nearly killed Beaver, who in the end succeeded in killing both. When nearly dead, Rat-Man called out, "I have two caches! The good meat is in the eastern one, and the poor meat in the western one." Beaver went to the eastern cache, and saw that it contained dried human flesh. He burned up the two caches and also Rat's lodge, and all the implements which he used for killing people.

Beaver continued his journey down the river, and came to the place where Kingfisher lived. He lived by spearing fish, and did not kill people. Beaver hid his canoe, changed himself into a large salmon, and swam to the place where Kingfisher used to draw water. Kingfisher saw him, and ran back to get his spear. He returned quickly and speared the salmon; but his spear-point broke off, and the fish swam away with it. Kingfisher was very sorry to lose his spear-head. He went back and sat down. Soon Beaver came along in his canoe. He had the spear-head hidden in a box in the canoe, where it could not be seen. Kingfisher said, "O my friend! I have just lost a big fish that went off with my spear-head. Had I caught the fish, we should have eaten together. I should have cooked it for you." Beaver went up to Kingfisher's lodge, where his host made him fall asleep and then read his thoughts. He found out that the spear-head was in Beaver's canoe, and went to search for it; but he broke up the whole canoe before he succeeded in finding it.[1] When Beaver awoke, he went down to the canoe and found it broken. He reproached Kingfisher, saying, "I thought you said you were a good man and always treated your guests well. Now you have broken my canoe." Kingfisher said, "I wanted to get my spear-head, so that I may be sure to get food. If you are not satisfied, I will throw a sleep on you again." Beaver did not kill Kingfisher, because he was not a cannibal. He lived entirely by killing fish.

When Beaver was leaving, Kingfisher said to him, "You will find Otter-Man living lower down; he is a bad man, and eats people. Look out for him! He has a rope stretched across the river a little above the surface of the water, and any canoe which hits it is cut to pieces."

Beaver repaired his canoe and continued his journey. He watched for the rope. When he was near it, he lifted it up with a stick which he had taken aboard, and passed underneath. Some distance below

[1] See notes in RBAE 31 : 606, No. 67 (Bellacoola, Chilcotin, Comox, Fraser Delta, Haida, Kwakiutl, Loucheux, Shuswap, Thompson, Tlingit). The author inquired for this tale among the Tahltan, but did not find it. See also MAFLS 11 : 17.

he saw smoke on a point, put ashore, and came to the camp of Otter-Woman, who had in her privates animals that bit and killed men.[1] The woman ran down to meet him, and cried, "You must be my husband!" She hurriedly bundled his belongings into her game-bag, tied it up, and was about to carry it up to her lodge. Beaver said, "Stay! I want to drink some cold water. Will you fetch me some?" She hurriedly brought some water from near by; but Beaver said, "That is no good, it is too warm. Go up to the spring in the mountain and get some really cold water." When she had gone, Beaver cut one of the strings of the bag. Otter-Woman at once knew, and turned back. Beaver beckoned her to go on; and when she was far away, he cut the other strings of the bag, took out his belongings, and embarked in the canoe. He went downstream to an island where he made up his mind to camp over night. Otter-Woman came back, jumped into the river, swam to the island, and went to his camp. Beaver killed two beavers at this place for food. Otter-Woman took the skins, tanned and dressed them, sewed them into mitts for Beaver, and laid them by his side. Beaver and Otter-Woman staid on opposite sides of the fire. When Beaver awoke, he found the mitts the woman had made, and, looking across the fire, he saw her lying naked with her legs apart, in a tempting attitude. Beaver heated a stone, and, instead of having connection with her, he pushed the stone into her vagina and killed her. A weasel and mink came out, and he killed them.[2] These animals bit men who had connection with the woman, and killed them.

Beaver continued his voyage down the river. He saw the smoke of a big camp, and put ashore. Here lived Shrew-Woman, who was very small and very wise.[3] The smoke from her lodge rose out of the grass. She asked him where he was going and where he had come from. When he told her, she advised him not to go farther down the river. She said, "An evil being lives lower down. He is gifted with great magical power, and has many cannibal monsters under his control. Above his house are two huge snake-like monsters with hairy manes, that lie one on each side of the river.[4] When they sleep, their eyes are wide open; and when awake, their eyes are shut. When anything comes down the river, they both dart out their heads and seize and devour it." Beaver said he was hungry, and Shrew cooked a few

[1] See notes in RBAE 31 : 604 (No. 63), 614 (No. 12), 773, 809 (Arapaho, Bellacoola, Chilcotin, Comox, Dakota, Fraser Delta, Jicarilla Apache, Kwakiutl, Lillooet, Maidu, Pawnee, Sahaptin, Shoshoni, Shuswap, Thompson, Wichita [also in the Old World]). Also known to the Tahltan. See also MAFLS 11 : 17, 152.

[2] See Tsetsa'ut (Boas, JAFL 10 : 46).

[3] Compare many tribes where a mouse is an old woman noted for wisdom, and people ask her for advice, — a small black mouse among the Tahltan, the short-tailed mouse among the Shuswap. See Kwakiutl (for instance, JE 3 : 12), Tahltan, Thompson (MAFLS 6 : 64; JE 8 : 209), Tlingit (RBAE 31 : 838), Tsimshian (RBAE 31 : 752).

[4] See RBAE 31 : 797.

salmon-eggs for him in a tiny kettle. Beaver thought to himself, "That is not enough." Shrew read his thoughts, and said, "You will find there is enough." As the eggs cooked, they and the kettle grew bigger, and Beaver found he could not eat all.[1] When Beaver left, Shrew gave him two fish to throw, one on each side, to the snakes when he reached them. He came down midstream in his canoe; and as he approached the snakes, he saw that their eyes were shut. He then knew they were awake; and, as he passed between them, they darted out their heads to devour him. He threw a fish into the mouth of each; and while they were devouring the fish, he passed on out of reach. A short distance below this place he saw two girls, sisters, playing on the shore. He went ashore above them, and, changing into a bluebird, flew near them. The sisters thought the bird could not fly very well, and chased it. At last the younger girl caught it and carried it home. When they reached their lodge (they slept together, and apart from their parents), the elder sister offered to buy the bird from the younger one by paying her a silver spoon she owned. The younger one agreed, and they exchanged. The elder girl took the bluebird to bed with her, and placed it between herself and her sister. When she awoke, she found a young man lying between them, and the bird was gone. The girls began to cry, for they knew their father would kill the man.[2] They left him and went to breakfast. Their father noticed tears in their eyes, and asked them why they were crying. At last they told him of the young man, and he told them he wanted to see him. They brought the man to him, and he at once seized him and put him into a large kettle that he had on the fire. He kept him in there for two days boiling, then he lifted the lid to see if he were properly cooked. Beaver had changed himself into a little bird; and when the lid was lifted, he flew out and escaped.[3] The cannibal tried hard to catch him, but without avail. During the interval the sisters felt very sorry for the man and cried often. That night Beaver came to them and slept between them as a man. In the morning they cried again, for they knew that their father would try again to kill him. Their father heard them, and knew the man was there. When they went to breakfast, their father asked them, and they finally told him the man was there. He said to them, "All right, you may keep him as

[1] Compare incidents of the magic kettle or dish which cannot be emptied: Bellabella (Boas, Sagen 223, 227), Chippewayan (Petitot 369), Kathlamet (Boas, BBAE 26 : 103), Kwakiutl (Boas, Sagen 154), Lillooet (MAFLS 6 : 96), Micmac (Rand 24), Newettee (Boas, Sagen 181) Nootka (Boas, Sagen 103), Ponca (CNAE 6 : 138, 139), Shuswap (Boas, Sagen 4; JE 2 : 644, 648), Thompson (MAFLS 6 : 43; JE 8 : 221, 315). Also known to the Tahltan.

[2] See RBAE 31 : 797.

[3] See RBAE 31 : 806 (Tlingit, Haida, Tsimshian, Tsetsa'ut); also known to the Tahltan.

a husband, and he shall work for me." He told his son-in-law, "You must finish my canoe for me," and showed him a large, partly finished canoe, the sides of which were kept apart by a cross-stick. When Beaver went inside to work, the cannibal pulled out the stick, and the sides closed in and imprisoned Beaver.[1] The cannibal went home and told his wife that the strange man was dead or a prisoner. Shortly afterwards he returned to the canoe, and found it split and his son-in-law gone. Beaver had burst the canoe by spreading his elbows. Next morning the cannibal heard his daughters crying again; for they knew the difficult tasks their father would give to their husband, and that if he failed in any of them, he would lose his life. That day the cannibal told his son-in-law that he wanted some eagle-feathers for his arrows, and directed him to a big tree where the Bald-Headed Eagle lived, who ate people. Beaver climbed the tree, and found only two young Eagles in the nest. He asked them when their parents would come home; and they answered, "Our mother will come with wind and rain at noon, carrying the legs of a man. Our father will come with wind and hail in the evening, carrying the upper part of a man. He eats the rest." One of Eagle's children always told his parents everything. He therefore could not be trusted, so Beaver killed him. Beaver said to the other, "When your mother comes, tell her your brother got sick in the head and died; and you are sick in the head now too, and will die by and by if you eat any more of that meat she brings. You must not eat any of the meat. If she asks what it is that smells like a man around here, tell her it is only the smell of the game she brought." Beaver hid with a club outside the edge of the nest. When the Mother-Eagle arrived, she asked why her son was dead, and the boy told her all as directed by Beaver. He also refused to eat of the meat she had brought. The mother said, "Very well, I will eat the meat myself." When she had eaten just a little, a piece stuck in her throat and threatened to choke her. She then knew there was something wrong. Beaver jumped up and clubbed her, and threw the body away. Beaver told the boy to tell the same story to his father, and, if the latter asked where his wife was, to tell him she had not yet come home. When the Father-Eagle arrived, he asked for his wife. When he was told that she had not yet come, he said, "That is strange, she always arrives here before me." The boy refused to eat the meat he brought; so the father began to eat it himself, choked on it, and was killed by Beaver, who now descended, plucked the feathers out of the dead birds, and returned.[2] The cannibal was

[1] See RBAE 31 : 801 (Bellacoola, Chilcotin, Chinook, Comox, Coos, Fraser Delta, Haida, Kodiak, Kwakiutl, Lillooet, Newettee, Nootka, Quinault, Squamish, Thompson, Tlingit, Tsimshian).

[2] See BBAE 59 : 286 (Arapaho, Assiniboin, Beaver, Chilcotin, Chippewayan, Dog-Rib, Gros Ventre, Hare, Jicarilla Apache, Kutenai, Okanagon, Ponca, Sanpoil, Shoshoni, Shuswap, Sia, Thompson, Uinta Ute).

much surprised that Beaver had returned alive. Next day he told his daughters that their husband had to get sinew for tying the feathers on his arrows. When they told Beaver, he sent one of them back to learn where he had to go; and her father told her he had to go to the hairy cannibal monster who lived beyond Shrew-Woman's house. On the way Beaver called on the Shrew and told her of the task he had to perform. She said to him, "I will help you." They went off together; and when near the monster's place, she dug a hole for Beaver in which to conceal himself. The hair was worn off the monster's haunches through sitting on the ground. When Shrew drew near, the monster asked her what she wanted. She said, "I want you to help me. I am cold, and I want some of the long hair from your body to weave a blanket for myself." The monster told her to pluck some hair from his haunches. She pretended to pull the hair, and said, "The hair is too tough and coarse here, it will not pull out." He told her to try another place. She did so, and said the same. Finally she said, "The hair under your arm seems to be the best. I will pluck some from there." The monster said, "All right." She pulled out much of the hair from under the arm over the heart, and left a bare spot. Beaver then shot an arrow at this vital place and mortally wounded the beast, who immediately crawled into his hole or den. Shrew crawled in, and found he was dead. Shrew-Woman now had plenty of meat, and she cut out the sinew for Beaver, who went back with it. When Beaver brought home the sinew, the women were glad, and their father was very angry.[1] Next morning he told his daughters to tell their husband to get glue to fasten the feathers and sinew on his arrows. He sent one of his wives back to ask where to get it. Her father said, "Down there in the lake." There lived a monster-fish, probably a kind of pike or a sturgeon, that ate people as they went along the shore. Beaver took his spear and went to the lake and speared the fish, which moved the whole lake in his death-struggles. When he was dead, Beaver cut out the part used for glue from behind the dorsal fin, and returned home. The cannibal was now very angry, and said to his wife, "This fellow has killed all my pets that kill men, and my arrows are not yet made."[2] Next day he sent him for paint to paint his arrows with, and sent word that it was up the river where he had passed. As Beaver went by, he called on Shrew-Woman for advice. She told him that the snake-monsters he had passed coming down the river lay on the paint. She said she would assist him. She made a man of clay to throw into the middle of the river. She said, "When they see him, they will pounce on him,

[1] Kutenai (Boas, BBAE 59 : 105).
[2] See Beaver (Goddard, PaAM 10 : 235), Gros Ventre (Kroeber, PaAM 1 : 88–90), Okanagon (Gatschet, Globus 52 : 137).

and then you may steal the paint from underneath the tail of the one on this side of the river." Beaver brought back the paint. The cannibal now transformed his daughters into grizzly bears, and put them on a side-hill across the river. He pointed out the bears to his son-in-law, and said, "Do you see those bears across the water? Let us go and kill them! You will go on the top of the hill, I shall drive them to you, and you will shoot them." He gave his arrows to Beaver, who saw that none of them had heads. Beaver, however, was prepared for this, and had hidden two bone arrow-heads in his hair. When Beaver got to the top of the hill, he put the bone heads on two arrows. The cannibal drove the bears, and, when they came near the top, Beaver shot the headless arrows at them; but they all broke, and none of them penetrated.[1] He then fired the arrows with heads, and killed both the bears.[2] The cannibal was very angry, and chased him with a knife. As he could not run fast, he called on his wife, who was fleet of foot, to chase Beaver. When she had nearly caught up with Beaver, the latter made the ground crack behind him, and the woman fell down. Again she gained on him; but he reached a lake, jumped in, and changed himself into a beaver. The cannibal said to his wife, "You can run fast; go back and fetch my net, that I may catch him." The woman brought the beaver-net, and they set it in the lake. They tried for several days, but could not catch Beaver. The cannibal then called for the man (bird) with a big stomach [3] to come and drink up the lake. He came and drank the lake dry. Beaver then hid in the mud, and the cannibal and his wife probed all over for him. At last they felt him, and Beaver realized that he was in extreme danger. He called on Snipe, saying, "Quick! They have found me. Hurry and punch a hole in the stomach of that bad man (bird)!" Snipe approached the Bird-Man, who was sitting quite still on the edge of the basin where the lake had been. He was so full of water he could not move, and felt very heavy. He said to Snipe, "Don't come near me!" Snipe answered, "I shall not harm you. I am just looking for food near you." Snipe made a swift stroke with his bill, and punched a hole through Bird-Man's stomach and belly; and the water gushed out, and soon filled the lake.[4] Beaver began to swim about, and the cannibal and his wife rushed hurriedly away for fear of drowning. The woman told her husband to come home, saying he could not beat their son-in-law. On the way back they came to the bodies of their daughters, and began to cry. Beaver followed them, and, coming to the

[1] See RBAE 31 : 742 (Bellacoola, Chilcotin, Okanagon, Shuswap, Thompson, Tlingit, Tsimshian, Wasco); also Teit, MAFLS 11 : 79. Also found among the Tahltan.

[2] Also known to the Tahltan.

[3] A kind of bird. The narrator had forgotten the name.

[4] See BBAE 59 : 304 (Beaver, Chihula, Huron, Luiseño, Micmac). See also Lillooet (JAFL 25 : 333), Thompson (JE 8 : 254).

place, said, "Why do you cry? They are only sleeping." He said to the bodies of the bears, "Wake up!" and they arose and changed into the women they had been. They went off with him as his wives. The cannibal man was now powerless to do harm, and consented fully to his daughters marrying Beaver. Before they parted, he gave each of them a feather, which he told them to put in the water wherever they got their drinking-water. He told them that the feathers, although in the water, would always be dry as long as their husband remained faithful to them and did not go with other women, but the moment he was unfaithful the feathers would become wet. They were then to leave their husband and return home. Beaver went back to his own country,[1] and took his wives with him. The women examined the feathers every day, and knew that their husband was faithful. A long time afterwards Beaver met his former wife, who made love to him. He was unable to resist, and had connection with her. On the following morning, when his wives went for water, they found the feathers wet. They said, "We will leave our husband, for our father told us to do this.[2] Heat will come, and the people will suffer for this." Soon great clouds appeared, and the women disappeared in them.[3] Such a great heat came, that finally the water boiled. People jumped into the streams and lakes to cool themselves, and died. Beaver's first wife was the first one to die of the heat. Beaver put his brothers in a shady place, and covered them thickly with brush and grass to keep them cool. All the people died excepting Beaver and his brothers.[4] When the weather became cool again, Beaver made snowshoes for his brothers, and left them. He went off to search for his wives. He found their tracks and followed them. He found their old camps, with lynx-meat cooked by suspending it from a pole with hook and line before the fire. He did not touch any of the meat, and always camped off to the side. At last he came to a camp where the wood was still smoking. It was their last camp before reaching their parents. Beaver camped to the side of it. That night his father-in-law came into his camp and took up his place on the opposite side of the fire. Both men hung their trousers above the fire to dry. Neither of them spoke. In the night the cannibal interchanged the trousers, putting his own where Beaver's had been. Beaver arose

---

[1] Some say "in the sky;" others, "to the east."

[2] See RBAE 31 : 780 (Bellacoola, Chilcotin, Haida, Lillooet, Seshelt, Tlingit, Tsimshian), see also Tsetsa'ut (JAFL 9 : 267).

[3] Some people say "they ascended to the sky."

[4] See Bellabella (Boas, Sagen 216, 234; RBAE 31 : 886), Bellacoola (Boas, Sagen 246; JE 1 : 96; JE 10 : 87), Kutenai (Boas, BBAE 59 : 49, 67; VAEU 23 : 164), Kwakiutl (Boas, Sagen 157), Newettee (Boas, Sagen 173; CU 2 : 127), Shuswap (Sagen 5), Tsetsa'ut (Boas, JAFL 9 : 268), Tsimshian (Boas, RBAE 31 : 727). A similar tale is also found among the Tahltan ("Story of the Sun").

very early in the morning, threw the cannibal's trousers into the fire, and put on his own. When the cannibal discovered that he had no trousers, he said it would be very bad for him if the sun got up and he were without trousers. Beaver had two pairs, and the cannibal begged Beaver to give him one pair. When the sun was about to get up, Beaver took pity on him and gave him a pair, which he at once put on. The cannibal then acknowledged that Beaver was more powerful than he, and left him, ascending towards the sky.[1] Beaver watched where he went, and, following, came to where his wives were. He took them back, and travelled to where people were. After he had met them, they all travelled together. As they journeyed, two Ravens began to fly ahead of them. The Ravens drove all the game away, so that the people could not get any. It was winter, and they began to starve. When people died, the Ravens picked out their eyes. At last all the people had died excepting Beaver and his wives. The Ravens flew over them, saying, "Yes, you are alive yet, but it will not be for long. You will soon be dead too, and then we shall eat your eyes." The Ravens always flew ahead of them wherever they travelled, and at night roosted on a tree near by. It was moonlight, and Beaver burrowed under the snow until he was past the tree where the Ravens were sleeping. Then he ran ahead, and found the country full of caribou and other game that the Ravens had been driving ahead. He killed many caribou, and returned the way he had come.

Beaver now pretended to be dead to deceive the Ravens. He told his wives to put his hands up near his eyes and cover him with brush. The Ravens awoke at daybreak, and, looking down, saw that Beaver seemed to be dead. Beaver's wives left, crying. The Ravens flew over their heads, saying, "Yes, by and by you will be dead also, and we shall pick out your eyes." They flew back and alighted on the brush. Here they disputed as to which eye each would take. Beaver suddenly seized their legs, and they begged to be let off. Beaver, however, had no mercy on them, and burned them alive in the camp-fire, saying, "What about the people you have killed? Why should I spare you?" Beaver now went out to where he had killed the caribou. When he was about to return home, he smeared blood over his snow-shoes, so his wives would know that he had killed game.[2]

2. ORIGIN OF THE EARTH.

Once there was no earth. Water was where the earth is now. The world was as a great lake. The animals and birds wanted to have an earth, and proposed to dive for it. The earth was very deep under the

[1] Some people say "to the sky," for this cannibal was the Sun and lived there.

[2] The narrator said that there was more of this story, but he did not remember it. See BBAE 59 : 303 (Arapaho, Beaver, Blackfoot, Chippewayan, Comanche, Gros Ventre, Jicarilla Apache, Kutenai, Nez Percé, Pawnee, Thompson; see also Caddo).

water. Beaver and Muskrat, and all the animals and birds, dived, but none of them reached the bottom. None of them staid under water longer than half a day. At last Diver (a bird) went down. After six days he came up quite exhausted and speechless. His friends examined his toe-nails, and found mud or earth under them. From this they formed on top of the water a new earth, which grew until it formed the present earth. At first it was merely mud and very soft. Later it became firm, and trees and vegetation began to grow on it. Now the earth is old and dry. Perhaps it is drying up.[1]

3. THE GREAT FLOOD.

Once there came a great flood which covered the earth. Most of the people made rafts, and some escaped in canoes. Great darkness came on, and high winds which drove the vessels hither and thither. The people became separated. Some were driven far away. When the flood subsided, people landed wherever they found the nearest land. When the earth became dry, they lived in the places near where they had landed. People were now widely scattered over the world. They did not know where other people lived, and probably thought themselves the only survivors. Long afterwards, when in their wanderings they met people from another place, they spoke different languages, and could not understand one another. *This is why*

[1] The narrator stated that this was originally a long story. He had forgotten the cause ascribed for the Flood, its duration, and many etails that he had heard. Compared Algonquin (Charlevoix; see Barbeau, GSCan 80 : 295), Arapaho (Dorsey and Kroeber, FM 5 : 1, 3, 4, 6, 20 note), Assiniboin (Lowie, PaAM 4 : 101; Potts, JAFL 5 : 73), Beaver (Goddard, PaAM 10 : 256), Blackfoot (Wissler, PaAM 2 : 151; John Maclean, Canadian Savage Folk, p. 51), Carrier (Morice, TCI 5 : 10), Cherokee (Mooney, RBAE 19 : 239), Chippewayan (Petitot 378; Lowie, PaAM 10 : 195), Cree (Russell 206; Skinner, PaAM 9 : 83; JAFL 29 : 346; John Maclean, Canadian Savage Folk, p. 75; Petitot 472; Swindlehurst, JAFL 18 : 139; Simms, JAFL 19 : 340), Delaware (Chamberlain, JAFL 4: 210; Brinton, The Lenape and their Legends, p. 134), (?) Dog-Rib (Petitot 317; Sir John Franklin, Narrative of a Second Journey to the Shores of the Polar Sea [London, 1828], p. 292), Fox (Jones, JAFL 14 : 234; 24 : 209; PAES 1 : 363), Gros Ventre (PaAM 1 : 60), Hare (Petitot 147), Hidatsa (Maximilian Prinz zu Wied, Reise in das Innere Nord-Amerika 2 : 221), Huron and Wyandot (Barbeau, AA 16 : 290; GSCan 80 : 39, 48, 50, [Brébeuf] 293). Hale, JAFL 1 : 180; W. E. Connelley, Wyandot Folk-Lore [Topeka, 1899], p. 67), Iowa (cited by Boas, JAFL 4 : 15; Dorsey, JAFL 5 : 300), Kathlamet (Boas, BBAE 26 : 23), Loucheux (Camsell-Barbeau, JAFL 28 : 249), Maidu (Dixon, BAM 17 : 39), Menominee (Hoffman, RBAE 14 [pt. 1] : 114; AA [old series] 1890 : 243-258; Skinner, PaAM 13 : 259), Miwok (Kroeber, UCal 4 : 188, 202), Mohawk (Hewitt, RBAE 21 : 286), Newettee (Boas, Sagen 173, CU 2 : 223), Ojibwa (Schoolcraft, Hiawatha 39; Skinner, PaAM 9 : 175; De Jong, BArchS 5 : 14; Carson, JAFL 30 : 486; Jones, PAES 7 [pt. 2] : 151, 271, 405; A. J. Blackbird, History of the Ottawa and Chippewa Indians of Michigan [Ypsilanti, 1887]. p. 76; Radin, GSCan 48 : 20; J. G. Kohl, Kitschi-Gami [Bremen, 1859], 1 : 326, 2 : 224); Chamberlain [Mississauga], JAFL 3 : 150; for other Ojibwa references see Chamberlain, JAFL 4 : 193; Speck [Timagami], GSCan 71 : 36), Onondaga (Hewitt, RBAE 21 : 180), Sarcee (Simms, JAFL 17 : 180; E. F. Wilson, BAAS 58 [1888] : 244), Salinan (Mason UCal 14 : 82, 105), Seneca (Converse, Bulletin

there are now many different centres of population, many tribes, and many languages. Before the flood, there was but one centre; for all the people lived together in one country, and spoke one language.[1]

4. ORIGIN OF FIRE, AND ORIGIN OF DEATH.

Long ago the people had no fire. Of all the people, only Bear had fire. He had a fire-stone, with which he could make fire at any time. He jealously guarded this stone, and always kept it tied to his belt. One day he was lying down by the fire in his lodge when a little bird came in and approached the fire. Bear said, "What do you want?" and the bird answered, "I am nearly frozen, and have come in to warm myself." Bear told it to come and pick his lice. The little bird assented, and began to hop all over Bear, picking his lice. While doing this, it also picked the string which fastened the fire-stone to Bear's belt. When the string was completely picked asunder, the bird suddenly snatched the stone and flew off with it.[2] Now the animals had already arranged for the stealing of the fire, and waited in line, one behind another.[3] Bear chased the bird, and caught up with it just as it reached the first animal of the line. As it threw the fire to him, he ran with it; and, as Bear in turn overtook him, he passed it on to the next; and so on. At last the fire was passed to Fox, who ran up a high mountain with it. Bear was so exhausted that he could not follow Fox, and turned back. Fox broke up the fire-stone on the top of the mountain, and threw the fragments a piece to each tribe. Thus the many tribes all over the earth obtained fire; *and this is why there is fire in the rocks and woods everywhere now.*

Fox then descended to a creek and threw a stick down into the water, saying, "When people die, they shall come back to life again, even as this stick rises again to the surface of the water; also old people, when they die, shall come back young again." Just then Bear came there, and, feeling angry because the people had stolen his fire, he threw a

N.Y. State Museum 125 : 33), Shoshoni (Lowie, PaAM 2 : 19, 247), Yokuts (Kroeber, UCal 4 : 204, 209, 218, 229; Powers, CNAE 3 : 383; Potts, JAFL 5 : 73), Yuchi (Gatschet, AA [1893], 279, 280; Speck, UPenn 1 : 103). The author did not find this incident among the Tahltan, although he inquired for it. See also P. J. de Smet, Letters and Sketches (Philadelphia, 1843), p. 40, probably Cree; N. Perrot, Memoir on the Manners, Customs, and Religion of the Savages of North America (in E. H. Blair, The Indian Tribes of the Upper Mississippi Valley, 1 : 35), probably Ottawa.

Mr. Robert T. Aitken has kindly given me the following additional references: Iroquois (David Cusick, Ancient History of the Six Nations, p. 1), Montagnais (?) (LeJeune, Jesuit Relations 5 : 155, recapitulation 6 : 157).

[1] Compare Bellacoola (Boas, Sagen 243), Carrier (Morice, TCI 5 : 10), Comox (Boas, Sagen 95), Lillooet (Teit, JAFL 25 : 342), Makah (?) (Swan, Indians of Cape Flattery, 57), Squamish (Boas, Sagen 57), Thompson (Teit, MAFLS 6 : 20, 44; JE 8 : 333), Tsetsa'ut (Boas, JAFL 9 : 262), Tsimshian (Boas, Sagen 278, RBAE 31 : 243), Twana (Eells, Am. Antiquarian 1 : 70 [Clallam, Lummi, Puyallup]).

[2] See Tsetsa'ut (Boas, JAFL 9 : 262); RBAE 59 : 299, 301; Teit (MAFLS 11 : 2).

[3] See BBAE 59 : 301 (note 3).

big rock into the water on top of the stick, so that the stick never came up again. Bear then said, "Henceforth, when people die, they shall be dead always, and shall never come back again." If Fox's stick had come up again after being hit by the rock, Fox would have won, and people would have had their lives renewed each time they died. There thus would have been no real death.[1] Bear now, having no fire, said, "I will make a hole in the earth, so I shall be able to keep warm in the winter-time. I shall make my hole right on the trail." Fox said, "If you make your house right on the trail, people will always find you. Make it on the mountains." *This is why bears now make dens in the mountains.*

5. RAVEN, OR BIG-CROW.[2]

The Kaska have a story of Raven, who acts as a transformer and trickster. The story is not well known to most of them, and may have been borrowed, at least in part, from the Tahltan. My informant would not attempt the telling of this story, as he said he did not know it well enough, and none of the other Kaska who happened to be at hand knew it any better. Among the incidents in this story are those of Raven defecating and asking his excrements for information,[3] and of Raven sending his penis across a river, where it enters a girl. Muskrat called out, "Cut it with grass!" Adsit[4] thinks this incident may have been borrowed from the Cree, who have a story of the culture-hero getting Muskrat to swim across a river with his penis, which then enters a girl. The latter gets sick, and Muskrat calls out to cut it with grass.[5]

6. BIG-MAN (DÉNE TCŌ).[6]

Big-Man was in the world very long ago. He was of huge stature, and had no hair on his head. When he stood erect, his head touched the sky. Once a long time ago the sky was very close to the earth,

---

[1] See BBAE 59 : 303 (Arapaho, Assiniboin, Blackfoot, Caddo, Cheyenne, Coeur d'Alène, Comanche, Coos, Dieguño, Dog-Rib, Eskimo, Hare, Klamath, Kutenai, Lillooet, Maidu, Miwok, Pawnee, Pomo, Quinault, Sanpoil, Shasta, Shoshoni, Shuswap, Takelma, Thompson, Ute, Wintun, Wishosk, Yana; see also Luiseño). Also known to the Tahltan. Compare p. 486 of the present number of this Journal.

[2] There exist analogous Tahltan stories of Raven. — J.A.T.

[3] See BBAE 59 : 294, note 5 (Chilcotin, Chinook, Flathead, Kathlamet, Lillooet, Nez Percé, Okanagon, Shoshoni, Shuswap, Takelma, Thompson).

[4] George Adsit of Telegraph Creek, B.C., has lived for many years among the Cree, Kaska, and Tahltan.

[5] See MAFLS 11 . 71, 189; and RBAE 31 · 722 (Arapaho, Alsea, Assiniboin, Blackfoot, Gros Ventre, Kalapuya, Menominee, Molala, Nez Percé, Shasta, Shuswap, Thompson, Tillamook, Tututine, Wishram).

[6] See BBAE 59 : 289, note 2 (Caribou-Eaters [Etheneldeli], Dog-Rib, Kato, Kutenai). Similar tales occur among the Tahltan.

and therefore it was always cold weather. At this time there was no room for Big-Man. When he travelled, he had to crawl, for the sky was very low. After a time he became angry at this inconvenience, and began to push the sky up. He kept on pushing it up, until at last he was able to stand at full height. The sky was now high, and far from the earth, and this made the weather on earth much milder. Since then it has been as it is now. Big-Man was a good man, and never harmed Indians. Some think he went to the sky-world, or somewhere up above, and that the rain is his tears.

7. THE BROTHERS, BIG-MAN, AND THE GIANTS.[1]

Two brothers lived together.[2] The younger one hunted all the time; while the elder staid in camp, cooked, and kept house. The latter began to dislike his younger brother, and would not give him anything to eat when he came home.[3] One day the younger brother became very hungry, and killed a porcupine. He made a fire, and cooked it on a hook suspended from a pole near the fire. When it was about half done, a giant came, and the lad ran up a tree. The giant smelled of the porcupine, and threw it away. Finding the lad's snowshoes, he ate out the fillings. Then he began to chop down the tree in which the lad was. The lad cried for his elder brother, who went there at once. When the giant saw him approaching, he was glad, for he saw in him a meal. The elder brother offered to help the giant, and took the axe. He said, "That boy is very bad. He always does mean things. I will help you chop the tree, so that we may get him and eat him." He swung the axe with great vigor; and the giant, standing a little too close by, received a cut on the brow from the back of the axe. The man said to him, "Stand farther away, I might hit you hard." He chopped hard and wildly, swinging his axe around. He watched his chance, gave the axe a great swing, and, instead of hitting the tree, cut off the giant's head. The brothers opened it, and many mosquitoes flew out, which were his brains. *This is the reason why giants are so foolish and easily fooled, and also the reason that mosquitoes are in the world now.* Had they not opened the giant's head and let the mosquitoes out, there would be none of these insects now.[4] The elder brother cooked the porcupine, and gave half to his brother. After this, they shared equally when eating. Now they travelled on, and always camped in new country.

[1] The Tahltan have an analogous story of "Big-Man and the Boy."
[2] Some informants say that the two brothers left their father and went hunting. They were lost, and led a nomadic life.
[3] Compare Chilcotin (Farrand, JE 2 : 41), Lillooet (Teit, JAFL 25 : 314), Shuswap (Teit, JE 2 : 672). — J. T.
[4] In two Tahltan stories ("The Brothers and the Giant" and "The Man who fooled the Cannibal Giant") similar incidents occur.

They came to a region where there were no porcupines. They could not get anything to eat, and were famished. The elder brother became very hungry and very weak. At last he could travel no farther, so he camped in the snow and made a big fire. He thought he would kill his younger brother and eat him. The latter lay on the opposite side of the fire, and watched him. When the fire had been burning some time, the elder brother heard a sizzling noise on his brother's side of the fire, and went to investigate. He found that they had lighted their fire over the frozen carcass of a buffalo that had been killed fighting, and the side of the animal was cooking. They cut it up and ate some of it, and the elder brother became stronger. The younger brother now hunted and killed some fat buffalo, the ribs and inside fat of which he carried home and fed to his brother, who ate so much that he nearly burst. The younger one said to him, "Eat some more!" but he answered, "I cannot." The younger one said, "Eat more, be sure you have your fill. You thought of eating me." The elder answered, "My stomach was empty, that is why I thought that way; now I am full." They became good friends, and went on to a new locality.

One day, when travelling, they came to a porcupine's den in the rocks. They saw Big-Man approaching, and, never having seen him before, they were afraid, and went into the porcupine-hole. Big-Man asked them to come out, saying that he would not harm them. The elder brother came out, but the younger one was afraid and staid in. Big-Man was angry because the younger brother would not trust him: so he made the rocks grow together, and thus prevented him from getting out.[1] Big-Man told the elder lad that he wanted him to help him get back his wife, whom a giant had stolen. Big-Man had two large dogs which he used as pack-animals. They were the grizzly and the black bears.[2] Now the giant travelled, carrying the lad under one arm; and very soon they reached a different country, where everything was of enormous size. A very large kind of beaver formerly inhabiting the world was to be found here. The beavers had hairy tails. The giant and the lad reached a large lake in which there were many beavers. Big-Man caught them in nets. He ate them, and threw away the tails. The lad hid himself, and cooked and ate one of the tails. Big-Man asked him what he was eating, and the lad told him. Big-Man said, "Put some in my mouth, I want to taste it." When he had tasted the beaver-tails, he said, "That is the best food I ever ate," and he told the boy to gather all the tails he had thrown away.[3] Big-Man sent the lad out to scout. He said, "Look about and see if you can

---

[1] The rest of the story is similar to the Tahltan story, "Big-Man and the Boy." See the same story, Tsetsa'ut (Boas, JAFL 10 : 43).

[2] See RBAE 31 : 798 (Chinook, Fraser Delta, Nootka, Thompson); Shuswap (JE 8 : 636), Thompson (Teit, JE 8 : 365; MAFLS 6 : 34).

[3] Lillooet (Teit, JAFL 25 : 333), Thompson (JE 8 : 255). — J. T.

see a big lake with what looks like an island in the middle." Big-Man was fond of the lad, and always called him "Grandson." The lad went up on the top of a high hill and looked around. He saw what looked like an island in the middle of a lake, and returned to tell Big-Man. The latter said, "That is the giant fishing."

Now they prepared to fight the giant. Big-Man made bow and arrows and spear, and the boy made a beaver-tooth axe. He intended to take a large beaver-tooth for the axe, but found he could not lift it, so he took a young beaver's tooth. Big-Man told the boy to go near the lake and to bark like a dog. He said, "The giant will become frightened and run home. You follow him up, barking, and I will lay in wait for him on the trail between the lake and his house." The fish the giant was catching in the lake were all covered with hair. When he heard what he thought was a dog barking, he put his pack of fish on his back and ran for home. When he came close enough, Big-Man fired an arrow at him; but the giant jumped aside, and the arrow missed him. Then Big-Man attacked him with the spear, but the giant evaded the thrusts. Now they seized each other and wrestled. After a long time Big-Man became weak, and called on the boy for help. The latter ran up, and, striking the giant with his beaver-tooth club, hamstrung him, and he fell down. They then killed him.

Now they went to the giant's house. When the giantess saw them, she called out, "Why did you kill my husband?" She threw huge rocks at Big-Man, but the latter jumped aside and avoided them. The giantess stood up and put her breasts on Big-Man's shoulders. They were so heavy, he nearly fell down. They wrestled; and the boy cut the sinews of her legs as he had her husband's, and she fell down.[1] They killed her and her babies and all her children. The babies were of the size of tall men. Big-Man took back his wife, and thanked the boy for his help.

The boy wanted to return to his own country and see his parents. He had been away a long time. He knew his country was far off, and he did not know where it was nor how to reach it. Big-Man knew his thoughts. He said, "I will give you one of my dogs to ride. When you get out of food, kill him and eat him; but be sure to preserve one arm-bone, and keep it close to your head when you sleep. It will be bare when you fall asleep; but when you awake, it will be clothed with meat. Thus you will always have food to eat. I shall also give you a walking-stick. When you retire, always stick it up near the head of your bed. In the morning you will find the stick pointing a certain way, which will be the direction you must follow for that day. Thus you will know your road. Some morning when you find that the stick has fallen down and is lying flat, and your bone is devoid of meat, you

[1] Kathlamet (Boas, BBAE 26 : 92), Micmac (Rand 196).

will know you are near your destination, and will reach home that day." Big-Man also told him that he would not see him again, but that he would know by signs when he died. He said, "When I die or am killed, you will see the sky all red: that is my blood. You will also see rain fall: that is my tears." Big-Man gave him his grizzly-bear dog to ride. The lad had only gone a little way when the bear began to growl and wanted to fight him. He called back to Big-Man, who changed the dogs, and gave him the black bear to ride.

He went on until he came to a country where there was no game, and became hungry. Then he killed the bear and ate it, but kept the bone, as advised. One morning when he awoke, he saw that the stick had fallen down and that there was no meat on the bone. He was glad, and he reached his parents that day. *That is why black bears are much better eating than grizzly bears, and also why grizzly bears are mean sometimes and want to fight people.* That is also probably *why people say that bears were originally dogs.*

Not long afterwards the lad saw the sky all red, and rain fell. He then knew that his friend Big-Man was dead. *That is why people say now that a red sky is blood* (or Big-Man's blood); and *when rain falls, it is tears* (Big-Man's tears).[1]

8. THE GIANTS AND THE BOYS.

Two boys were stolen by a giant, who gave them to his wife to fatten for him. He hunted beaver all the time, and killed plenty; but he was very fond of human flesh, and preferred it. He always told his wife to cook something nice for him, meaning the boys; but she always cooked beaver-meat, as she liked to keep the boys to help her fetch water and do other things. At last she thought her husband would some time get angry if she did not take his suggestions: so one morning early, after her husband had gone hunting, she woke up one of the boys and told him to take the buckets and go for water. She wanted him to be absent, so that he would not know that she had killed his brother.

As soon as he left, she pulled off his brother's penis, and then killed him. The lad heard his brother's cries, and knew what had happened. He kicked the buckets to pieces, and then went back to the house, where he called, "Give me the arrows! I see a grouse on the water-trail!" She gave him the arrows. He broke them to pieces, and then ran away. As he did not return, the giantess went to see what was keeping him so long. When she saw the buckets and arrows broken, she called to her husband, who came back and started with a spear in pursuit of the boy. The boy hid in a crevasse of a glacier, where ice was piled up. The giant was too large to enter, and he could not

[1] Tsetsa'ut (Boas, JAFL 10 : 46).

break the ice: so he poked in the hole with his spear, thinking he could thus kill the boy. The boy rolled up his blanket and put it to one side. The giant thought this was the boy, and kept stabbing it. The boy hit his own nose and made it bleed, and rubbed the blood on the spear-point. The giant thought he had killed the boy, so he left his spear there and went home. He told his wife, "You killed one for me yesterday, and I have killed one for you to-day." She had already cooked the boy's privates and his body, and now the couple ate all except the bones.

The giant told his wife, "We will shift camp to where the other boy is, and eat him next. When they reached the ice, he told his wife to crawl in and bring out the body. She crawled in, and found nothing but blood-stains. The giant said, "His body is certainly there. Where are your eyes?" His wife then pointed out the broken spear, and they knew that the boy had escaped. After feeling around in the hole, the giant started in pursuit.

The boy reached a place at a large lake where there was a large camp of people fishing. They made ready all their weapons, and sharpened many sticks. When the giant arrived, he asked, "Has my grandson come here?" and the people answered, "Yes, he is here." The giant said, "His grandmother weeps for him, and I have come to get him." He asked the boy if he would come back; and the boy answered, "Yes." The people invited the giant in, asked him to be seated, and gave him fish to eat. After eating, the giant asked the boy to louse his head. The boy loused his head. The people stuck the sharpened sticks into the ground all round, and the boy tied the ends of the giant's hair to the sticks. While the boy was lousing his head, the giant thought of eating the boy, and pierced his leg with a bone. The boy jumped away, and the giant reached out to catch him. As he did so, he found that his hair was tied to pegs all round, and that he could not arise.[1] The people then attacked and killed him.

The giant had told his wife to follow him. The people made a new camp on the way she was to come, and prepared to receive her. They cooked the fat from the stomach of her husband, and had it ready for her. When she arrived, she was carrying a bundle, and pretended that it was a baby. She herself cried, imitating a baby. Then she would say, "The baby is not crying: I am doing this to fool the Indians." She asked where her husband was, and the people told her he was at the camp beyond, but would soon be back. She answered, "My husband is not in the habit of going to other camps." The people had already told her the camp she was now in was made by her husband especially for her. They assured her that her husband would be back soon, and said to her, "Sit down, and we will give you

[1] Chinook (Boas, BBAE 20 : 18).

something good to eat." She sat down on the pretended baby. The people asked to see her baby; but she said, "It cries when anybody looks at it." The people gave her her husband's fat to eat. She said it had a bad taste, and they told her it was perhaps a little old. She began to eat again. Some of the people went behind her, and tied the ends of her hair to the neighboring willow-bushes while the others spoke to her and entertained her. When all was ready, they began to laugh at her, and said to her, "That was your husband's fat you ate." She got angry and opened the sack she carried, in which were stones for throwing at the people. The people attacked and killed her. When they opened the bundle to look at the baby, they found only the bones of the boy she and her husband had eaten.

9. BLADDER-HEAD BOY; OR, THE MONSTER THAT ATE PEOPLE.

A man with his wife and baby were travelling all the time, and netting beaver on the lakes and streams. They came to a big lake, which they crossed, and camped on the other side. One day the woman was dragging to camp a skin toboggan with beaver-meat, carrying her baby on her back. She noticed some large animal approaching, and, being afraid to turn around, looked back between her legs. She saw that the animal was an *a.tix'*,[1] and became very much afraid. She scattered all the meat in the snow and ran to camp. Her husband would not believe that she had seen this animal, and told her she was simply excusing herself for having given the meat to her sweetheart. She pulled up her clothes, and said, "You can see I have been with no man." He laughed, and went off to set his beaver-nets. On his return, he went to bed, and was soon sound asleep and snoring. The woman cut a trail to escape through the willow-brush near camp. She then lay down on the opposite side of the fire from her husband, with her moccasins on and her baby in her arms, ready to run. During the night she heard the animal coming, and poked her husband with a stick to awaken him; but he slept on. She then ran away, and the animal came into camp and ate her husband. Afterwards the animal followed the woman's tracks, making sounds like a person crying.

The woman reached a place on the lake where many people were camped, and warned them. The people made many holes close to-

[1] A very large kind of animal which roamed the country a long time ago. It corresponded somewhat to white men's pictures of elephants. It was of huge size, in build like an elephant, had tusks, and was hairy. These animals were seen not so very long ago, it is said, generally singly; but none have been seen now for several generations. Indians come across their bones occasionally. The narrator said that he and some others, a few years ago, came on a shoulder-blade which they at first thought was a peculiarly shaped rock, sticking out of the ground. This was on the top of a mountain near the Hyland River. The shoulder-blade was as wide as a table (about three feet), and was covered with about seven inches of moss.

gether in the ice of the lake, so that the animal, in approaching, would break through and drown. When it came to this place, the ice broke with its weight; but the animal walked along the bottom of the lake, broke the ice ahead of him, and came out to where the people were. The woman with the baby ran away. The other people were so scared that they could not run. They fell down quite helpless, and some of them were as if asleep.

In the camp was a boy who was ill treated by everybody. Even the old women stepped over him, and treated him as if he were a dog. He looked as though he had no hair, because he wore a moose-bladder over his head. Only his grandmother knew that he was like a shaman. He had magic trousers and magic arrows. Now, his grandmother nudged him, and said, "See what is coming!" He said to her, "Get my trousers and arrows." He donned his trousers and seized his bow and arrows. He jumped, and shook his head. The bladder burst, and his hair fell down over him. He shot an arrow right through the animal. Then he jumped to the other side and shot an arrow back through it again. Thus he shot until he killed the animal. The people were very thankful, and gave him two girls to be his wives, but he accepted only one of them. They made him their chief. *This is why since then people have had chiefs.* The woman who ran away came back again.

10. THE KASKA MAN WHO MADE WHALES.[1]

A Kaska man was married to a Tlingit woman, and lived near the ocean. His sister lived in the same village, and was married to the brother of his wife. Beyond, out in the ocean, was an island of ice just like a glacier, and no one had ever been able to climb it. The people were hunting seals near there in a large canoe. They said, "The Kaska are good climbers; they are an inland people. We should like to see our son-in-law try to climb up on the island." The Kaska man said he would try. He put on his snowshoes and snowshoe-spurs, took his walking-stick with spiked end, and landed. He did not have much difficulty in climbing the ice, and soon reached the top. The Tlingit were jealous, and shouted loudly; then they turned the canoe and paddled away. A boy on board, who was his brother-in-law, was sorry, and paddled the opposite way to the other paddlers, for he did not want to desert him.

The Kaska man felt very sad when he saw that he was deserted, and finally lay down on the ice and fell asleep. It seemed as if he dreamed,

---

[1] See RBAE 31 : 818 (Haida, Rivers Inlet, Tlingit, Tsimshian). Also known to the Tahltan.

For the incident of the invisible arrow see RBAE 31 : 820 (Bellabella, Bellacoola, Comox, Coos, Haida, Kwakiutl, Lower Fraser River, Nass, Newettee, Nootka, Tlingit, Tsimshian).

but it was reality. Some one spoke to him, and asked him to come down underneath. He went down into a house which was the Seal people's house, and saw many people there. They asked him how he had come to be asleep overhead, and he told them. One of the Seal men was sick. He had been speared by a Tlingit, and the harpoon-head was in his flesh. The shamans of the Seal people did not know what was the matter with him nor how to relieve him. They had tried all kinds of treatment. Some of them proposed that they ask the stranger to try and cure him. The Kaska man knew at once what was the matter. He blew on the wound, and then pulled out the harpoon-head without any difficulty. All the people were glad. They asked the Kaska if he wanted to go home, and he said, "Yes," They put him in a distended seal-bladder, the neck of which they tied securely, and then set him afloat in the sea. They told him he must think only of his home. If he thought of anything else, he would immediately return. When he hit the sand and heard the noise of the waves on the shore, he would know he was at home, and might then open the bladder and get out. When he had reached half way to his destination, he thought of the place he had left, and immediately went back. The people warned him again, and sent him forward. Several times this happened. At last he managed to concentrate his thoughts long enough on his home, which he now reached very quickly. He sent back the bladder to the Seal people as soon as he got out of it. He told his wife of his experiences, and asked her not to tell any one.

Now he went in the bush near the seashore and carved a number of pieces of wood in the shape of whales, and threw them into the water end first. All of them were too light, and bounced up too quickly. He tried all kinds of wood. At last he made them of a hard heavy wood. When he threw them into the water, they went down a long way, and rose to the surface afar off. He transformed them into whales and sent them to catch seals. When they accomplished this, he called them back. He said to them, "Now, you must go to meet the large canoe with the seal-hunters, overturn it, and smash it; but you must spare the boy, and leave him a piece of canoe to float on." The Whales did as directed, and all the seal-hunters were drowned excepting the boy.[1] He called the Whales back, and said to them, "Now you shall be real whales, and go in the ocean as you will. You shall overturn canoes sometimes, and shall also eat seals. You shall be the largest and strongest animals of the ocean." *This is why the Tlingit say it was a Kaska man who created the whales.*

[1] For the making of the artificial whale see RBAE 31 : 822 (Haida, Nass, Tlingit, Tsimshian); and the making of artificial animals or of swift canoes (Comox, Haida, Lkuñgen, Nass, Newettee, Nisqually, Quinault, Tlingit, Tsimshian; also Thompson [Teit, JE 8 : 272]).

Kaska Tales. 453

11. WAR WITH THE SWAN PEOPLE.[1]

Once a man had a wife who had many brothers. He hunted caribou all the time, and his wife staid in camp and prepared the meat and skins. One day when carrying caribou back-fat, and while on his way home from hunting, he heard cries from down below, near his camp. He hurried there, and found that a strange man had taken his wife. She had held on to the willows, but he had dragged her along and put her in his canoe. He was just pushing off when the husband arrived at the water-edge. The husband told the man to let him see his wife; but the man would not do this, and kept her down in the bottom of the canoe. The husband asked the stranger many questions; and the latter answered freely, for he thought there was no possibility of his ever being followed. He learned that the stranger was a Swan man. He belonged to the Swan people, who often stole women from the Indians. They lived in a high cold country a long distance off. Between their country and the Indian country the sky intervened; but at intervals it would rise for a short time, and then fall again on the water. At these times people could pass through from one country to the other. The man stated that there was snow in his country already, and that the winter had set in. The husband asked him how he did on the way going home. He answered, "I anchor my canoe with a stone every night, and go on in the morning." The husband then asked him to give him something that would satisfy him for the loss of his wife, and he gave him an arrow. Then the stranger departed, never expecting that people could possibly follow him.

The husband now gathered all his own friends, his wife's brothers and all her friends, to make up a large war-party. They made many canoes, many snowshoes, many moccasins, and many arrows and spears. They started on the track of the Swan man over the lake. At night they lashed all their canoes together and anchored them. After many days they arrived at a place where there seemed to be a hole in the sky. The sky was rising and falling at short intervals at this place. They watched a chance when the sky rose above the water, and rushed through. The sky came down and hit the last man. They thought this bad luck: so they gave this man a canoe, and sent him back.

It was summer in their own country, but on the other side of the sky it was already winter. At last they saw smoke on the shore, and came to an old camp. The people had lately left this camp, excepting two old women [2] and a girl. They had gone off on their early winter

---

[1] The narrator said he thought the scene of this story was somewhere near the ocean or a very big lake. The last part of the story is called "The Child Story," but he did not remember the details of it.

[2] Some informants say that the women were very old and blind, and therefore not able to travel with the people.

hunt in the interior. The war-party hid near the camp. One old woman said to the other, "Put a stick on the fire." She got up and pulled a log along to put it on the fire. One of the war-party, concealed in the bushes near the fire, took hold of the opposite end of the stick. He pushed it and pulled it, causing the old woman (who held on) to go backwards and forwards. The other woman laughed, saying, "Why does she go back and forth in that way?" The woman holding the log made a sign to her to keep quiet, and not to laugh. Then she whispered, "Maybe there is some one here. You know there was a woman stolen by our people lately."

The war-party now cached their canoes, put on their snowshoes, and followed the people's tracks. They intended to kill the old women on their return. The Swan people were still travelling every day, the men hunting, and the women dragging the toboggans and making the camps. The captive woman had not slept with her new husband yet. She always lingered behind, dragging her toboggan; and when she cut brush for the camp, she always did so back on the trail. An old woman also followed behind, being unable to drag her toboggan as fast as the others.

The husband who had lost his wife was chief of the war-party. After a number of days they caught up with the Swan people, and the chief went ahead to reconnoitre. He saw his wife cutting brush, and he stopped. She came back along the trail, and saw him. She was glad, and about to rush towards him; but he said to her, "Don't come near me, only speak! We are famished. Can you get food for us?" The old woman was not far away, and she had much meat in her toboggan. The captive woman went to her, and told her how her axe had broken, and that she wanted some sinew to tie the stone to the handle again. The old woman said, "Go to my toboggan and take out some sinew." She went there, and took out meat and replaced it with brush. She then hauled the meat back to the war-party. Again she hauled back brush to camp, and told the old woman her axe had broken again. The old woman told her to take some more sinew, and she took meat and carried it to the war-party. The chief (her former husband) said to her, "To-night put fresh meat on the men's snowshoes and on their arrow-points (and spear-points?), so that it will freeze on, and they cannot use them. In the morning a strong wind will blow, and then we shall come. Keep your husband [1] awake by playing and fooling with him until he is tired. He will then sleep soundly."

Her new husband was chief of the Swan people. When nearly daybreak, the woman built a fire, and one man started out to hunt. Then a strong cold north wind began to blow, and nothing could be seen

---

[1] Some people say "two husbands."

outside the camp except the driving snow. The war-party crept up in the storm, and the woman ran out and joined them. They attacked and killed all the people. The only one who escaped was the man who had gone hunting.

When they returned to the camp near where they had cached their canoes, they found that the two old women and the girl had changed into mice. They set out on their return journey on the lake, and came to the place where sky and water met. They found that the sky had frozen to the water, and that they were barred by what seemed a wall of ice. All the shamans and the animals tried to make a passage through, but without result. The Lynx jumped at the ice wall, trying to make a hole with his nose, and drove it back into his face. *This is why he has now such a short blunt nose.* At last Weasel made a hole and passed through; the next animal, a little bigger, enlarged the hole and went through; and thus they enlarged the hole, a bigger animal passing through each time. At last the moose went through, and then they took the canoes through.[1] The party then travelled back the way they had come, and reached home in safety.

Now the Mice women in Swan land travelled into the interior to find their people. The girl with the old women was sister to the man who had gone hunting and thus escaped death. They found his tracks and followed him; but he always kept ahead of them, and camped alone. They could not overtake him. The old women had a dog that could speak like a person. This dog always went forward to the hunter's camp, and brought back meat for the women and the girl. Thus they continued journeying until they reached a large camp of Swan people who were their friends. The hunter would not camp with them, however, because his sister (the Mouse girl) was pregnant, and he was ashamed. He had never had connection with her, so he was much ashamed when people said he was the father of his sister's child. He became so much ashamed that he committed suicide. (Here follows the child story, which I did not record.)

12. THE DESERTED WOMAN.[2]

A man and his wife were travelling with other people. The woman had a heavy load, and was following behind. She came to a hill where the people had slid down with their toboggans on the snow. Here she found a ball of fat which must have been lost from one of the toboggans. When she reached camp, she showed the fat to her husband. He became angry, and accused her of having a sweetheart, which she denied. He said, "Your sweetheart must have paid you in

---

[1] See Tsetsa'ut (Boas, JAFL 9 : 261).

[2] See Thompson (Teit, JE 8 : 237). The Tahltan have an analogous story of "The Deserted Woman."

fat." (*This is why some married people are now suspicious of each other, and accuse each other of infidelity without sufficient reason.*) In the morning the husband burned his wife's clothes and tools, the people extinguished the fires, and all of them deserted the place, leaving the woman to die of cold and starvation. Only her sister-in-law had pity on her, and told her she had left a little fire for her in one place.

As soon as the people were out of sight, the woman blew on the embers left by her sister-in-law, and made a small fire. Numbers of rabbits began to come to the deserted camp. She found some scraps of sinew at a place where the men had been making arrows. She made a snare with these, and caught a rabbit. She took the sinews of its legs and made another snare. Thus she continued catching and living on rabbits. She made needles and awls of their bones, thread of their sinews, and clothing and blankets of their skins. She took great care not to let the fire go out, as she had no axe or any tools for making fire. She collected whatever fire-wood she could find. She had no snowshoes, and could not go very far, for the snow was deep in that place.

At last March came, and spring was near. There was a hard, thick crust on the snow. One day she tapped on her knee, and said, "I wish some of you people would come this way!" She said this almost without thinking, as if in fun. Soon afterwards a moose ran past the camp, and a man on snowshoes in pursuit on the crust. Seeing the moose had passed near the camp, the man asked the woman how long since it has passed or how far ahead it was. She pointed out to him the branches of a tree still moving which it had touched in passing, and made a sign that it had just gone out of sight. The man went on, after telling her that his brother was following and would camp there that night. The brother came along, following the tracks, and, seeing the camp, left his blankets there with the woman. The first brother killed the moose, and that night both brothers returned to the woman's camp heavily laden with moose-meat. They cooked meat and gave some of it to the woman. During the course of the evening they asked the woman why she was alone, and why she wore only rabbit-skin clothing, and she told them all. They said, "When we return to our camp, we shall tell our mother." They told their mother, who said, "I am almost blind now, and I am very glad you have found this woman. She will be a wife for you, and will sew your clothes." They took the woman to wife, and she made for them fancy clothes of moose and caribou skin, embroidered richly with quill-work, and feather head-dresses. (*This is why men are now jealous of a good wife, who looks after them well and makes fancy clothes for them.*) She also made good clothes for herself. (*This is why men now like a woman who dresses neatly and well.*)

The woman staid with her husbands and mother-in-law in one place. After a time her former husband arrived, and, finding tracks, he followed them to the camp. He was surprised to find his former wife there, finely dressed, well provided with meat, and having two husbands. He offered to buy her back with a stone axe and arrows. The woman took the axe and threw it into deep water, and threw the arrows into the fire. She said to him, "Don't you remember how you left me to starve? I shall never go with you now!" He departed crying. (*This is why, when a good woman separates from a bad man, she becomes better off, and never returns to him.*)

13. THE SISTERS WHO MARRIED STARS.[1]

Once two sisters made camp together, and before retiring looked up at the stars. They saw two particularly brilliant stars, — a red and a white one. One sister said to the other, "I shall take that red one for my husband, and you may take the white one." That night, when asleep, they went up to the stars, and awoke next morning in the sky, each with a man by her side. The sister who had chosen the red star was covered with a red blanket belonging to the man with whom she slept, and the man of the other sister had a white blanket. The women lived with these men in the sky-world, as they knew no way of getting back. Their husbands hunted every day, and killed plenty of game. Thus they had an abundance of food.

The women decided to try and get back to earth. They cut up skins and made a very long rope. When their husbands were away hunting, they worked at digging a hole in a hidden place in the timber. At last they dug through, and could see the earth beneath. They tied a stone to the end of the rope and let it down, but the rope was too short. By adding rope to rope they at last found that the stone reached the earth. They made many pairs of gloves to wear while sliding down the rope, to prevent friction on the hands and to guard against the rope getting worn out. One day when their husbands were away, the younger girl slid down and reached the earth, and the elder followed her.

When the men returned from hunting, they searched for the women, and, finding the hole and rope, they threw the latter down. The sisters found they had alighted on the top of a large tree near a main trail where people were constantly passing. They saw the Moose, Wolf, and many others pass. As each one passed, he called, "My brother-in-law is coming behind!" At last the Wolverene came in sight, carrying his snare on his back. (*This is why the wolverene now has*

[1] See BBAE 59 : 309 (Arikara, Assiniboin, Blackfoot, Caddo, Chilcotin, Dakota, Gros Ventre, Kutenai, Micmac, Otoe, Pawnee, Quinault, Sanpoil, Shuswap, Songish, Thompson, Tsetsa'ut, Wichita; see also Arapaho, Crow). Known to the Tahltan.

the peculiar marks on his back like a snare.) When he arrived under the tree, the women whistled, and he looked up. When he saw the women there, he was glad, and climbed the tree. When he reached them, he wanted to have connection with them; but they said, "Take us down first!" He carried one of them down, and then wished to have connection with her; but she said, "Bring my sister down first." He ascended and brought down the other woman. Then he wanted to have connection with both; but they told him, "You must provide us with food first, for we are hungry." Wolverene went off and stole dried meat from somebody's cache. When they had eaten, he demanded again to have connection with them. They told him, "Our father advised us never to have a man unless he was able first to provide fat caribou-meat. You cannot expect to have a woman until it is certain you are able to kill fat caribou." He went off hunting, and the sisters fled. They ran until they came to the canyon of a river, which they were unable to pass. They sat down, and before long they saw Wolverene coming. He was carrying a heavy pack of fat caribou-meat. As soon as he arrived, he wanted to have connection with the women, without even waiting to take his pack off. The sisters knew what he would do when he reached them, and had arranged that one of them would pretend to let him have connection, and the other one would then kick him over the cliff. One woman lay down near the edge of the cliff, and he went to have connection with her. She told him the right way to do was first close his eyes and fold his arms. The other sister then kicked him over the cliff into the river below. The women then ran along the canyon to a narrow place, where a large man (who was a kind of snipe) aided people in crossing. There was very bad water (rapids) in the river at this place. They called on the man to help them cross; and he stretched his long legs across, and they walked over on them. They said to him, "We will pay you porcupine-quill garters if you will let Wolverene drop into the river. When he comes, just stretch one leg across, and turn it when he is half way over." He agreed, and they gave him the garters. Wolverene came along, carrying his pack. He said to the man, "Where did you get my garters? I will kill you if you do not help me to cross at once." The bird man stretched one leg across for him to walk on. When he was half way over, he turned his leg, and Wolverene fell into the river and was drowned.[1]

The sisters went back to their parents, and lived with them. They told their parents, "When we travel, you must go ahead and make bridges for us over every creek, and even over every swampy place and wet spot." Their father always did this. At last one time, feeling tired, he neglected to bridge one little spot. The sisters never came

[1] Crane bridge. See Waterman (JAFL 27 : 43); Blackfoot (Uhlenbeck, VKAWA 13: 130); Sahaptin (MAFLS 11 : 177).

to camp, and their mother went back to look for them. She found that they had turned into beavers, and had already built a house. After this they were beavers.

14. THE MAN WHO COHABITED WITH HIS SISTER.[1]

A man lived in one place with his two wives, who were sisters. The elder had four children, and the younger none. In another place not far away lived his sister, who was married to a brother of his wives. The man always killed plenty of marmots, and the family were well provided for. After a time he brought home no marmots, and the family began to be hungry. He had become enamoured of his sister, who was a young girl, and he visited her constantly. He killed his sister's husband (brother to his wives), cut his body open, and defecated inside. He brought all the meat to his sister, and none to his family, for he wished them to starve to death. He claimed that he had bad luck and could get no game. Sometimes he was away as long as five nights, and returned without anything. The women managed to live by snaring ground-squirrels. They noticed that their husband was always fat and contented-looking, and he never slept with them. They became suspicious, and one day the elder wife followed him. When he was out of sight, she ran; and when in sight, she lay and watched. She took advantage of the nature of the ground, and followed him until she saw him enter his sister's camp. She hid and watched until she saw him leave the camp for the purpose of visiting his marmot-traps. He was dressed in new clothes, while, when he came home to them, he always wore old ragged clothes. When he was out of sight, she approached the camp, and, in passing by the place where they got water, she saw the defiled body of her brother lying there. She entered the camp, and saw much meat there. She said to her sister-in-law, "Oh, you are well off! Your husband must be a good hunter, for you have plenty of meat on hand. Our husband cannot get anything, and we are starving." Her sister-in-law then cooked some liver for her, although there was an abundance of good meat in the camp. After eating, she said to her sister-in-law, "I think you have many lice in your head. I will louse you before I go." The girl accepted the service, and laid her head in the woman's lap. After lousing her a little while, the woman took the two bone scratchers which were suspended by a string around the girl's neck, and with one in each hand ran them into the girl's ears and killed her. She pounded up some dried meat, and filled the girl's mouth and nostrils with it. Then, taking a pack of the best meat and fat, she went home, and fed her children with fat. When the man returned to his sister's camp, he found her dead, and was very sorry. He took his

[1] Also known to the Tahltan.

pack of marmots to his own camp, where he said to his wives, "I have had good luck this time, and have brought you some meat; but you must make a camp for me some distance away, as I want to be alone. If I sleep with you, my bad luck may return." His real reason was, that he might be alone, and thus be able to cry without being noticed. The women made a camp for him a little ways off, arranged everything nicely, and put a block of wood under his pillow. That evening they fed the children with some roots. One of them cried for fat; and the women, fearing their husband had heard it, said, "It is roots the child means. How could he know about fat? He has never been used to eating it."[1] Their husband went over to his camp, and they could hear him crying. After a while he fell asleep, and they could hear him snoring. The two women then went over and clubbed him to death on the head. Before he died he cried, "You have killed my sister, and now you kill me!" (*This is why men sometimes take a fancy to their sisters, and even cohabit with them.* Had not this man in mythological times become enamoured of his sister, men would not do so now.)

The elder sister now proposed that they should go to where their late husband's brother lived, and tell him what had happened. He was unmarried and lived alone. The younger sister was afraid, saying that he would kill them; but at last she agreed to go. They gathered all their meat together, and took all the marmots from the traps, and made a cache of all. Then they burned the body of their husband and departed. When they drew near their brother-in-law's camp, the elder sister said, "I am not afraid. I don't care if he kills me. I shall go and see him." She went into the camp, carrying her baby on her back, and told the man of the killing of his brother and sister, giving him full details. He said to her, "You have done right. My brother did evil, and acted like a dog." The woman told him that her sister was afraid, and remained some distance away with the children. He said, "Tell her to come in. She need not be afraid. I do not blame you for what you have done." She went into camp with the children, and the two sisters became the wives of their brother-in-law.

15. STORY OF THE WATER-MAN.[2]

Some people who lived near a lake were troubled by a water-man who lived in the middle of the lake. He fooled and ate people. In the centre of the lake could be seen numerous very long strings, like weeds, on the surface of the water. This was his hair. On the edge of the lake was a thing growing, in substance like a stick, and in shape like a man's penis. This was his penis. The people had tried many

[1] See Eskimo (Nelson, RBAE 18 : 467); Russell (JAFL 13 : 15); Jetté (JAI 38 : 341).
[2] Tsetsa'ut (Boas, JAFL 10 : 48).

times to break it, but could not accomplish it. They practised bathing in cold water to make themselves strong, so that they might break it, but without avail. Among the people who were making medicine that they might attain power to break it was an orphan boy who lived with his uncle, who had two wives. His uncle and the younger wife treated him badly. Each succeeding night the boy tried to break the penis, and at last one night he accomplished the feat. He put it together again, and said nothing. Next morning his uncle, accompanied by many men, went to try again, and it broke easily.[1] All were glad, and went back to camp rejoicing. They composed a song on the occasion. They thought they could now conquer the water-man.

Next morning they went in a large canoe to kill the water-man. The boy's uncle stood in the prow of the canoe to do the killing. When they embarked, he had told the boy to go home, as he would be of no use; but the boy went, nevertheless, and sat in the stern of the canoe. His uncle seized the water-man by the hair, and was about to strike at him, when the latter moved his head; and he fell out of the canoe, and was at once killed by the water-man. The boy then arose, and, running forward to the bow of the canoe, seized the water-man's hair and killed him. He struck off his head as easily as cutting fat. The people then returned, singing a song of victory and a death-chant together. The boy's uncle's wives heard the singing, and began to paint themselves, as they thought their husband was the victor. The elder was doubtful as she heard the two kinds of songs; but the younger one kept on painting herself, although the paint constantly scratched her face. The boy had made it do this.

When all the people learned of the boy's victory, they made him chief, and he became renowned throughout the country. He took his uncle's elder wife to be his wife, but would have nothing to do with the younger one.[2]

16. THE DECEITFUL WIFE.

A woman had two husbands [3] who were brothers, and their mother lived with them. She and her mother-in-law shifted camp while her husbands went hunting. When about to make camp, she noticed that she had forgotten her needle-case in the last camp, and she went back for it. On her return she fell in with a war-party of many men, who intended to attack her people. They had connection with her until she became quite exhausted. They told her not to tell the people, gave her a lot of ptarmigan, and let her go. She carried the birds to camp and gave them to her mother-in-law. The latter asked her

---

[1] See Tlingit (Swanton, BBAE 39 : 145, 289).

[2] A Tahltan story, "The Deserted Orphan and the Goat Chief," is similar to the end of this story.

[3] Notice the common reference to women with two husbands in Kaska. It appears also in Tahltan myths. This does not occur in any Salish stories that I have collected.

how she came by them, and she told her that she had killed them with stones. The old woman examined them, and saw that they had been killed with arrows. She said to her daughter-in-law, "Get some water for your husbands; they will be coming home soon." When she had returned with the water, she immediately lay down and slept, for she was very tired. Just when the men were coming, the old woman spilled the water, then woke up her daughter-in-law and sent her for more water. She noticed that she was very lame. While she was gone, the woman showed the birds to her sons, who at once knew there was something wrong. They had brought home some fat cariboumeat. They told their mother they would have a last big feed together, and that when the meal was finished she must go out and try to escape. They cooked and ate a hearty meal. When the repast was over, the old woman took the pails, pretending that she was going for water. She left the camp, and ran off into the woods. The men built up a huge fire so as to intensify the darkness surrounding it. They then attacked and killed their wife, because she had deceived them. The war-party heard her cries and rushed into the camp. The brothers ran out in the darkness and escaped. *This is why since then women have been deceitful and hide their actions and wrong doings.*

17. THE OWL-WOMAN.[1]

A woman lived with her daughter, who had two husbands who were brothers. She was visited by two men who, she thought, were her sons-in-law. She made up her mind to get rid of her daughter and have her sons-in-law for herself. She told her daughter to climb up a tree where the owl lived, and get some owl-feathers for her. Her daughter refused, saying that she was afraid she might turn into an owl; but her mother persuaded her that there was no danger. When half way up the tree, the girl's clothes dropped off, and feathers began to grow on her, and she became an owl. The old woman dressed in her daughter's clothes, fixed up her face and hair to make herself look young, and then sat down in a new camp she had made to await the coming of her sons-in-law. After they came home, she remarked as she was eating, "I am young yet, see how sharp my teeth are!" and again, as she got up, "I am young yet, see how quickly I can get up! I am like a young woman." The men noticed that she got up slowly like an old person; and this, with the remarks she had made, caused them to be suspicious. They pulled back her head and her hair, and recognized her as their mother-in-law.[2] Thinking she had killed their wife, they killed her, and then went to their old camp. On the way they passed the tree where their wife was, and saw her.

[1] A similar story is found among the Tahltan.   [2] See RBAE 31 : 605 (No. 64), 861.

Kaska Tales.

They begged of her to come back to them; but she answered, "No, you have killed my mother, so I shall remain an owl."

18. THE DOG-MAN AND DOG-CHILDREN.[1]

A family consisting of parents and daughter lived together. They had an old dog who always lay at the entrance of the lodge. Whenever the girl went outside, she had to step over the dog. One day they moved camp, and as usual put a pack on the dog. When they reached the camping-place, the dog was missing. The parents sent the girl back to look for him. She met a good-looking man accompanied by a dog carrying a pack. He asked her where she was going, and she told him she was looking for their dog, who had gone astray with his pack. He answered, "This must be your missing dog. I found him, and am bringing him along." The girl, becoming fascinated with the man, ran off with him, and camped in a different place. The man hunted, and always obtained plenty of game. He told his wife, "When you throw away bones, never throw them far." The woman noticed that when her husband hunted, she always heard barking where he was. She asked him about this, and he answered that he knew nothing of the barking. She also noticed that the bones she threw out were always eaten up or gone in the morning.

One night she pretended to sleep, and watched. Her husband arose, and soon afterwards she heard something eating the bones outside. She looked, and saw that it was an old dog. She now knew that her husband was a dog or dog-man, and, taking a club, she struck the old dog on the head and killed him. She then went back to her parents and told them she had been living with a man, and that she was pregnant. Her mother, thinking she would have a nice baby, prepared for it by making a fine marten-skin robe, and a nice bed for the baby to be born in. The girl gave birth to seven pups; and her mother became so angry and disgusted, that she snatched away the robe, took away all the food and everything in the lodge, and left the place. Her father and all the people also deserted her.

[1] The narrator said that he thought this story may have come from the Tahltan to the Kaska some time ago, as both tribes have the story localized in the Tahltan country. See RBAE 31 : 785 (Bellacoola, Chilcotin, Comox, Kwakiutl, Nootka, Quinault); Carrier (Morice, TCI 5 : 28); Cheyenne (Kroeber, JAFL 13 : 182); Chinook (Boas, BBAE 20 : 17); Dog-Rib (Petitot 311; Franklin, Second Voyage, p. 308); Eskimo (Rink, Tales and Traditions of the Eskimo, 471; Boas, RBAE 6 : 630; Murdoch, American Naturalist, 1886 : 594; Boas, JAFL 7 : 207; Holm, Meddelelser om Grönland 39 : 270); Fraser Delta (Boas, Sagen 25; MAFLS 11 : 130); Hare (Petitot 314); Kathlamet (Boas, BBAE 26 : 155); Lillooet (JAFL 25 : 316); Squamish (Hill-Tout, BAAS 1900 : 536); Thompson (Teit, MAFLS 6 : 62, JE 8 · 354, MAFLS 11 : 30); Tlingit (Krause, Die Tlinkit Indianer, p. 269); Tsetsa'ut (JAFL 10 : 37); also Coos (Frachtenberg, CU 1 : 167). Known to the Tahltan.

The girl lived by picking berries. When their mother was away gathering food, the pups turned into children and played together. There were six boys and a girl, and the girl always watched while the others played. The mother noticed, when she came home, that the brush on the floor of the lodge was disturbed and turned over, as if children had been playing; and she thought it strange that dogs should do this. She picked up some rags and made them roughly to resemble clothes, which she stuck up within view of the lodge one day when she was out. The girl watched this, thinking it was her mother. The latter crept around behind, seized the dog-skins the children had discarded, and threw them into the fire. The girl, however, managed to get on part of her skin, and thus remained half dog. Later the mother managed to get the rest of her skin, and she then became like her brothers.

The dogs were now really children, and they grew up fast. The young men hunted, and always brought back plenty of game. They had the power of scenting game, as dogs do, and therefore were very successful in hunting.

Now, the mother was suspicious that one of her sons slept with his sister, and she determined to find out which one it was. She smeared pitch all round where her daughter slept, and next morning she noticed the side of her youngest son marked with pitch. She was sorry about this, and began to travel with her family. When about to cross the Stikine River in the Tahltan country, she said to the girl, "Look at your brothers bathing in the river down below!" As soon as she looked, all were changed to stone, including the mother. Some were ashore at the time, and some were in the river. All of them are now rocks to be seen at this place.[1]

19. STORY OF LYNX-MAN.[2]

Once a long time ago a man was hunting in the mountains with his wife. At that time there was no game in the low parts of the country. People lived on sheep, marmots, and ground-squirrels, all of which abounded in the mountains. The man wanted to procure some eagle-feathers: so, taking a rope with him, and accompanied by his wife, he went to a cliff where there was an eagle's nest. He tied the rope around his waist, and got his wife to lower him down. Just when he had reached the ledge where the nest was, Lynx-Man appeared at the brink of the cliff, and ordered the woman to let go the end of the rope. Being afraid, she did as directed. Lynx-Man then took her away to a place in the bottom-lands where the brush was very thick and there were many Jack pines. Here he set many snares, and always caught plenty

[1] Tsetsa'ut (Boas, JAFL 9 : 257).   [2] A similar story occurs among the Tahltan.

of rabbits. He cooked and offered the woman rabbits, but she would not eat. On the way to this place the woman had carried some grouse that Lynx-Man had caught, and, as she went along through the brush, she plucked the birds and dropped the feathers along the way as a sign.

When the Mother-Eagle came back to the nest, she found the man there. She said, "What are you doing here?" and he answered, "I came here to get some eagle-feathers. My wife let me down, and I had barely reached the ledge when for some reason the rope fell down. Now I have no means of getting up or down." Eagle said, "Why, Lynx has stolen your wife; that is why the rope fell down. Get on my back, and I will take you down and show you where to find your wife." The man did not answer, as he was afraid, and Eagle knew it. She said, "There is no danger. I am able to carry you. Put that big stone on my back, and I will show you." The man did as directed, and the Eagle flew away with the stone on her back, and threw it off on the opposite mountain. Returning, the man got on her back, and she flew down with him.[1] Eagle then said, "Watch my flight. I will fly to where your wife is. When I circle four times, you will know she is directly below where I am." Eagle flew off, and the man watched. After flying some distance, Eagle circled twice, and then went on. After a time she circled four times, and then returned. On arriving back, Eagle asked the man if he had noticed where she went, and he answered, "Yes." Eagle then told him there was a large Caribou below where she had circled twice, and his wife's camp was underneath where she had circled four times. Eagle plucked a number of feathers from her body and gave to the man, saying, "I will now leave you. My children are hungry, and I must go and feed them."

The man went to where the Eagle had circled twice, and found a caribou there, which he killed. He then went on, and came to Lynx's camp, where he found his wife alone. She was glad to see him, and said to him, "When Lynx comes, you must say you are my brother, and address him as brother-in-law." Towards evening Lynx came to camp, carrying a load of rabbits. When he saw the man, he drew his bow and was about to shoot at him. The woman cried out, "This is my brother come to visit me. Don't shoot at him!" Lynx said, "Oh, my brother-in-law indeed!" and came into camp. He cooked many rabbits for his supposed brother-in-law. That night, when Lynx-Man was asleep, the man and woman killed him. Then they shifted camp to where the carcass of the caribou was.

[1] See Sanpoil (Gould, MAFLS 11 : 108), Thompson (Teit, JE 8 : 371).

20. THE FOG-MAN.[1]

A man and his wife were out hunting. They had two daughters who staid in camp. There was little to eat; and the girls, being hungry, ate about half of the back-fat that remained in the camp. Their mother was angry when she returned and found that they had eaten so much fat. She said to them, "Go up in the mountains and marry Fog-Man. He is a good hunter, and always has plenty of fat." The girls ran away from home, and, going up in the mountains, came to the place where the Fog people draw water. They met a woman there who was the mother of Fog-Man. The girls told her their story, and she said she would tell her son.

Fog-Man had two wives, Porcupine and Beaver. They were bad women. They ate people, and they were always angry and cross. As soon as Fog-Man learned of the girls from his mother, without saying anything, he arose and hit Porcupine with his axe, and drove her from the house. He said, "Go up to the timber-line among the balsam and become a porcupine. People will eat you." Then he hit Beaver with a stick, and drove her, too, from the house. He said, "Go down to the river and become a beaver. People will eat you also." He brought the girls in, and now had two good wives. He hunted and put up a great quantity of meat of caribou, sheep, etc., and fat ground-hog. He made a very big cache of meat in the mountains. Then he went to visit his parents-in-law, taking his wives with him, and plenty of meat. He staid a long time with his wives' people; and while he remained there, the people always had plenty to eat, for Fog-Man was a good hunter. His chief food was sheep's horns, which he called fat, and cut just like back-fat.

Each of his wives bore him a son. One day some of the people quarrelled with him, and he left them. On his way home he put a mountain on the top of his meat-cache, so that the people could not get at it. They could find no game, and were starving. They went to the cache to get meat, but were unable to remove the mountain which covered it. The woman (viz., mother-in-law) sent Fog-Man's sons to look for their father. She said to them, "When you see your father's tracks and follow them, paint the soles of your feet with red paint, and never look back." They did as directed, and found their father. Many Fog people were living there. When they went in, they gave the lads sheep's horns to eat.

When Fog-Man heard that the people were starving, he was sorry. He went to the cache and took the mountain off the top. The people now had plenty to eat. Fog-Man's mother-in-law ate so much fat, that she became too full, and, when reaching over to take some more,

[1] The Tahltan have a similar story ("Ca'kina"). See Tlingit (Swanton, BBAE 39 : 222, 280).

she broke in two.[1] After this, people used caches and put up meat in caches. Fog-Man taught them. *This is why the Indians now cache their meat and make caches.*

21. RABBIT-MAN (GA'.TCOEZE').

Rabbit-Man was very clever. He was a shaman and next in power to Beaver. He had two brothers and a sister. The latter was married to Bear-Man, and the two brothers lived with them. Rabbit lived alone in another place.

Bear became angry because his young brothers-in-law were lazy, and he made up his mind to starve them. He made them always camp behind himself and his wife, in a different place, and gave them raw liver. Rabbit-Man knew that his brothers were badly treated, and went to see them. He saw that his brothers had no fire and no good food to eat. After making a big fire for them, he asked where Bear-Man was camped. They said, "On ahead," and indicated the spot. Rabbit went to Bear's camp, and found only his sister (Bear's wife) there. He saw much fat meat there. Without saying a word, he helped himself to the meat, and went back and fed his brothers.

When Bear came home, he missed the meat, but said nothing. As he changed his moccasins, he thought of Rabbit. He knew that he had come, and he knew that he was a very clever man. Soon afterwards Rabbit appeared, and asked Bear if he had seen any moose or buffalo when hunting, and Bear replied that he had seen three. Rabbit proposed that they should go after them at once; but Bear said that he was too tired, and could not go until morning. At last Rabbit persuaded him to go that night. They chased the moose (or buffalo) and killed two. One ran off, and Rabbit went after it. He ran it down, killed it, and cached the meat in the snow.

On returning to Bear, he told him that he had failed to catch the runaway. Bear prepared to pack the two animals they had killed by tying them together, while Rabbit was to go ahead and break a trail for him to follow. Bear said, "My load is very heavy; break a good trail for me, and pick good easy ground." Rabbit made a trail through bad places and straight up steep places. At last he went up a very steep place, and Bear became angry. He said to himself, "I will fix him when I get to camp!" When Bear reached the top of the declivity with his heavy load, his head was bent down, and he was out of breath. Rabbit hit him on the head with a club and killed him. He rolled over backwards with his heavy pack. Rabbit then returned to camp, and told his sister, "Your husband wants you to meet him. He is tired." She answered, "No, my husband never yet asked me to

[1] Tsimshian (Boas, RBAE 31 : 825).

meet him." Rabbit persisted in the truth of his statement, and at last she went. He killed her at the same spot where he had killed her husband.

Rabbit now returned to his brothers, and took them to the place where he had cached the meat. There they camped, and cooked and ate much. Now, Bear-Man had many friends, and they came to take revenge. Rabbit gave each of his brothers a feather. He told them, if they were attacked, never to move or to say anything, but just to watch his eyes. He said, "While I sit, you sit; and when I get up, you get up." The Bear people came and attacked the camp. Rabbit got up; his brothers did the same, and all changed into feathers.[1] They blew away on the wind, and came down a long ways off, where they changed back to their natural forms and camped. Rabbit hunted and killed many moose, so they had plenty to eat. He said to his brothers, "Live here until I return. I am going to kill our enemies."

Rabbit arrived at the camp of an old Bear-Man, who was sharpening sticks.[2] He said to him, "Why are you making these sharp sticks?" and Bear answered, "To kill Rabbit-Man." (Bear did not recognize Rabbit, for he had changed his appearance.) Rabbit asked old Bear-Man how he used the sticks, and the latter showed him. Rabbit took up the stick, and, pointing it at Bear's head, said, "Oh, this way!" and then pierced him with it, killing him.

Rabbit went on to a camp of many people near a lake.[3] Changing himself into a young rabbit, he sat down near the hole in the ice where the people got water. Some women carrying water saw him and caught him. They took him to camp and showed him to the other people, who thought it strange that there should be a young rabbit in the middle of winter. They all examined him, passing him from hand to hand. Wolverene was the last one to examine him. After looking at him very closely, he said, "Perhaps this is Rabbit-Man," and threw him into the fire. Rabbit jumped out of the fire, and ran away as if lame. The people followed him, trying to catch him. He ran out in the middle of the lake, chased by the people. He made a gale of wind come and blow all the snow off the ice, which became so smooth and slippery that the people could not stand up. He then took a stick and killed one after another.

Wolverene had not followed him. He thought himself smart, and sat in the camp smiling to himself. Rabbit entered, and, striking him across the arms and legs, broke them. He put his body on a spit and set it up before the fire to bake. He then gathered all the children together, chinked up the brush lodge, and set fire to it. When all were

[1] See Chilcotin (Farrand, JE 2 : 24, 25), Thompson (Teit, MAFLS 6 : 74, 75; JE 8 : 265). — J. T.
[2] See Lillooet (Teit, JAFL 25 : 295), Thompson (JE 8 : 226, 227). — J. T.
[3] Also known to the Tahltan ("Raven and Qᴇxtsā'za"). — J. T.

burned up, he went home. *This is how wars started among the Indians.* At one time war was unknown. Rabbit introduced war, and the Indians imitated him. Since then there has been war among tribes and families. Had Rabbit not introduced war, people would know nothing of war now.

22. WOLVERENE.[1]

Wolverene had two wives and several children. His wives' mother, and two brothers of his wives who were yet boys, lived with them. He always caught many beavers, and gave plenty of meat to his mother-in-law and brothers-in-law as well as to his own family. He was very quick at setting beaver-nets, for he used his penis as an ice-chisel. The boys tried to find out how he managed to set the nets so quickly, but he always managed to conceal himself when making holes in the ice. One day, however, they happened to see him, and made remarks about the shape of his ice-chisel. One of his own sons told him of these remarks. He became angry, and said he would starve them. After that he fed his own wives and children, as usual, but gave nothing to his mother-in-law and brothers-in-law. He allowed them a fire, however, but he gave orders to his wives not to give them any food.

When Wolverene's daughter saw that her grandmother was starving, she went to her mother, saying she was very hungry, and asked her for some beaver-meat. Pretending to eat the meat, she passed it down her dress, and carried it to her grandmother and the boys. The latter now began to hunt, for they were very hungry. One day they chased a moose by the place where Wolverene was working beaver on the ice. They asked him if the moose was far ahead; and he answered, "Just a little ways." The lads chased the moose a very long way before they caught up with it and killed it. They brought back some meat and fat to their camp. That night they broke some bones to extract the marrow, and Wolverene heard them. He called out, "Oh, you have some meat! You are eating marrow-bones." The old woman was angry, and answered back, "No, you are mistaken. We are breaking old bones. Where should we get meat? We are starving."

That night, when Wolverene was asleep, the old woman and boys shifted camp to where the moose was. Next morning Wolverene noticed that there was no fire at their camp, and sent one of his sons over to find out the reason. He came back and told his father that there were no people there. Wolverene knew now that the lads had killed the moose. He made up his mind to follow them, and told his wives to go ahead. He would stay behind and finish catching beavers, and then overtake them. He killed a number of beavers, and, taking one of them on his back, he set out. Before long he passed his wife, who was pregnant, and therefore walking very slowly.

[1] Also known to the Tahltan ("Wolverene and the Brothers").

When he reached the people's camp, he said, "I have brought you some good meat;" and he gave the beaver to his mother-in-law. He had defecated inside the beaver. The old woman threw it away, saying, "We do not eat your dirt." Wolverene said, "How nice the moose-fat smells!" The people said, "We will feed you fat; sit down and close your eyes." He was not particular now about concealing his privates, but sat down before the fire and lifted up his apron (or shirt?), exposing himself to view. When he shut his eyes, the people poured hot grease on his privates. He began to scratch at the burnt place; and while he was doing this, they clubbed and killed him. They then went out and met the wife who had the children and was pregnant, killed her, and cut open her belly. They also killed all the children excepting the youngest, who managed to escape and climbed a tree. Here he became a wolverene, and said, "*Henceforth I shall break into people's caches, and steal out of their marten-traps.*"

23. WOLVERENE AND HIS WIVES.[1]

Wolverene married the eldest of many sisters, and took her to his house. He hunted all the time, and always had plenty of meat and fat. He had a hole in the ground under his house, into which he put his wife. He kept her there, and fed her just fat meat and fat. He never gave her any water to drink. When she was very fat, he killed her and ate her (or cached her meat). He then went crying to his mother-in-law's house, saying that his wife was dead. He cried so much, that they took pity on him, and he got the next oldest sister for a wife. He did the same with her. Thus he married and killed all the sisters excepting the youngest two.

At last the youngest sister of age was given to him. She thought something was wrong, and was on her guard. He treated her the same way. When she had been some time in the hole, she asked him why he had never slept with her; and he answered, "I don't want to spoil my food." She then told him to give her something to kill mice with, for they were annoying her terribly. He gave her a long, sharp piece of antler. While he was absent hunting, she dug a tunnel with the tool, until she got out to the bank of the creek. She was too fat to walk, so she rolled to the creek and drank. She then rolled onto a log, and floated downstream to the place where her mother drew water. Her sister, a little girl, came for water, and saw her. She went back and told her mother, who said, "Don't say that you saw your sister! She is dead." However, she went and brought her daughter up to the camp. She fed her nothing but water, so that she might get thin.

Wolverene thought she had died, and shortly afterwards appeared,

[1] See Eskimo (Boas, RBAE 6 : 633; Rink, Tales and Traditions of the Eskimo, 106; Holm, Meddelelser om Grönland 39 · 235), Shuswap (Teit, JE 2 : 702).

crying, and saying that his wife had died. The woman's mother hid her. Wolverene smelled her, and sniffed, saying, "Ah! What do I smell? It smells like an old cache." Then he thought his wife might have escaped somehow, and went back to see if she was still in the hole or cache. He was wont to leave his victims in the hole for a time after they were dead. His brothers-in-law followed close behind him. When he went into the hole to see if his wife was there, they hid close to the edge. When he stuck his head up to come out, they hit him and killed him.

24. WOLVERENE AND WOLF.

Wolverene and Wolf were brothers-in-law and lived together. Wolf had no wife, while Wolverene had a large family. They hunted in company, Wolf traversing the high mountains, and Wolverene following the timber-line below him. Game was very scarce. By and by the deep snow prohibited their hunting on the high grounds, and they had to hunt lower down in the woods, where game was still less abundant. One day they came on a cache of dried meat made by some people (Indians) in a bad precipitous place near a waterfall, and beyond their reach. Wolverene was very anxious to get at the cache, and thought by jumping against it he might knock it down. Wolf would not attempt it, and declared that if Wolverene jumped, he would not reach the cache, and would simply fall down on the steep, smooth ice below, and perhaps kill himself. Wolf declared he was going home, and, just as he was leaving, Wolverene made the jump. He fell short of the cache, landed on the steep ice, and was precipitated to the bottom, breaking his arms and legs. Wolf lifted him up; but he could not get him out of there, nor set his broken limbs. Soon afterwards some people came along to get meat from the cache, and found Wolverene lying there with his arms and legs broken. They knew he had been trying to steal, so they clubbed and killed him. As he was dying, he said to the people, "No matter if you kill me, I shall steal from your caches just the same. There are many of us." *This is why the wolverene is now such a thief, and breaks into people's caches and steals their meat.* Wolf returned to camp, and reared Wolverene's family.

25. STORY OF THE BABY STOLEN BY WOLVERENE.

A man and his wife were travelling towards where the people lived. The woman was taken in travail, and, as was the custom of the people, she had to go in retirement during and for some time after her confinement. When they camped for the night, the husband made a camp for himself, and another for his wife some distance away.

One night a giant came to the woman's camp, threw a noose around her neck as she was sitting at the fire, choked her, and dragged her body away in the snow. The baby, which remained alone, began to cry. The husband called out to his wife, "Why does the baby cry so much?" Receiving no response, he went over to see. When he arrived, the baby was quiet, and he found Marten suckling the baby with his tongue. He asked him what he was doing; and he said, "I am suckling the baby with my tongue, for his mother is dead." The husband took his bow and arrows and followed the giant's track in the dark, and after a time came to where the giant had lighted a big fire and was about to eat. He saw him sucking the milk out of the woman's breasts, and then he put them on sticks before the fire to cook. The man crawled up close to the giant, and fired an arrow into his body. The giant immediately put his hand up to the place, and said, "My! A spark has burned me!" He said to the fire, "Why did you do that?" Again the man shot him, and he did the same. Then he said, "It is strange, I feel sleepy." He lay down, saying, "I will sleep a little while before eating the breasts." He was dying, and did not know it.

When the man returned, he found Marten caring for the baby, and suckling him, as before. The man gave his breasts to the baby, and milk came. After that, in the day-time Marten suckled the baby with his tongue, and at night the father gave him his breasts. At last they reached the people, and the man gave his baby to the women to rear. He hunted, and every five days returned to see his baby, and was glad to see that he was doing well.

One day, when he was away hunting, Wolverene came to the camp and told the people the father had sent him to get the baby and take it to him. The people thought this strange, but gave him the baby. After five days the father came back, and asked to see the baby. The people said, "Why, don't you know, Wolverene came here some days ago, saying that you had sent him for the baby, and we gave it to him." The man stated that he had not sent Wolverene, and at once started in pursuit of him. At Wolverene's first camp he found baby-moss, his son being still a baby; at the second camp, small snowshoes, showing that the baby was now a boy and walking; at the third camp he found larger snowshoes, and saw that the boy had been using small arrows; at the fourth camp the snowshoes and arrows were larger; and at the fifth camp the tracks showed that the boy was now a man. Next day he found where the boy and Wolverene had separated, and he followed the tracks of the former.

The Wolverene always counted the lad's arrows when he returned home at night. When the man came to his son, the latter thought him very strange, for he did not remember having seen people. His father told him, "You are my son." He showed him his breasts, saying, "I suckled you. Wolverene stole you, and I have followed you a long way." The lad at last believed him. His father said, "Tell Wolverene, when you see him to-night, to follow the sun on the morrow, and camp where the sun goes down, and there you will join him to-morrow night. Also tell him that you shot an arrow up in a tree, and you are going back after it."

That night Wolverene counted the birds the lad had shot, and his arrows, and found one of the latter missing. Wolverene agreed to the boy's proposal. In the morning he travelled towards the setting son, while the lad returned. That night the lad did not come to camp, and next morning Wolverene started to look for him. He came to the lad up in the top of a tree, pretending to look for his arrow, and his father standing at the bottom. Wolverene asked the latter who he was, and what he was doing there; but when the man answered and talked with him, Wolverene told him to shut up or he would kill him. The father had already arranged with his son how they would act. Wolverene told the boy to come down out of the tree; but he answered, "Father, I can't descend, my moccasins are frozen to the tree." Wolverene said, "Very well, don't try to come down, you may fall. I will climb up and carry you down." When Wolverene got beside him, he turned around to get in position to carry him down, and the lad struck him on the head, knocking him off the tree. His father at the bottom of the tree then killed Wolverene, who was already stunned by the fall.

SPENCES BRIDGE, B.C.

www.ingramcontent.com/pod-product-compliance
Ingram Content Group UK Ltd.
Pitfield, Milton Keynes, MK11 3LW, UK
UKHW020747260225
4763UKWH00017B/451